runaway girl

V. Brown

Cover Design by Simply Defined Art

Edited by BLD Editing

Formatted by V. Brown

Content Warning

- Cheating on page (kiss only)
- Overheard betrayal
- Mentions of mental health & abandonment
- Graphic sexual content
- Strong language

Please take care of yourself, your safety and wellbeing.

Chapter 1

ALICIA

"What are we?" I asked.

Ethan froze beneath me; I could feel his muscles seize up from the dreaded commitment question as we lay naked together. I was half on top of him, our chests colliding with shortened breaths, and a fine sheen of sweat coated our skin after finishing round two.

Ethan didn't waste time in his escape, detangling himself from our position as he slipped to the end of the bed and collected his clothes.

"Why are you asking me this? You know what we are," he replied with an exasperated tone.

I followed his lead, redressing into casual clothes as if applying armour. "It's been four years since we started... whatever this is—"

"You said you agreed to this arrangement. We kept it secret for our careers. We're exclusive and don't hook up with other people, but we're not in any type of committed relationship. You said that worked for both of us," he snapped accusingly.

"And that did work for me. At first. I was invested in my career and had no time to spare for anything else. Our agreement worked well and still does."

"So what's the problem?" he asked, his blue eyes shifted to mine, a fire stirring within.

"Things have changed, Ethan. I'm twenty-eight, and I'm only getting older. I want *more.*" I didn't know why he was surprised; this particular conversation was well overdue.

"More? I don't do well with ultimatums, love."

"And I don't do well with burying my head in the sand and not voicing what I want."

"And what do you want, Alicia?"

"I want to be in a committed relationship. I want a loyal partner. I want to introduce them to my family. I want to get married. I want to have kids one day. I want a life filled with happiness. That's what I feel will make me happy."

"Wow, you really did bide your time well, didn't you?" he said with a cocky, condescending grin. Then, the asshole began a slow, dramatic clap. "Well done, Alicia. You really had me fooled. Played the long game and thought you could hook yourself a rich, big-time athlete, huh?"

"Get over yourself." I scoffed. "You may be the highest paid running back in the league, but *I'm* the one who's made you rich." I was one of the top-performing financial advisors at Stella Financial Management, and Ethan was my client. He wasn't about to undermine my role and the effort I put into my job.

Ethan sneered with an elitist air as he turned for the exit. "Oh, so now I owe you? This is brilliant. Next, you're going to tell me how much you've fallen in love with me, right? How you can't live without me? How I will never find another woman like you?"

Each word came out more scathing than the last, almost mocking in its deliverance. What made it worse was that he didn't even look at me while making those statements. Ethan merely strolled down the hallway towards my front door like we were discussing the weather.

I was struck dumb. Standing behind him, literally lost for words. It wasn't how I envisioned our "talk" to go down. Sure, we had a mutual agreement which was beneficial for both of us, but that was *four fucking years ago*.

I thought he would at least hear me out, and we could discuss our future like adults. Even if that meant we would move on separately, as individuals. I knew that was a strong possibility with Ethan's abysmal communication skills and commitment issues, but I wasn't afraid.

Heat raised beneath my skin as red filtered into my vision, alongside those pesky tears that always threatened to make an appearance when I was overcome with emotion.

I *hated* that *fucking crying* was my body's natural response, like my faculties were being overloaded with too much stimulus that it had no choice but to leak from my eyes. Even when all I felt was frustration and anger.

And right then, I had that in abundance.

Ethan wrenched the door open and spared a glance over his shoulder. "Oh, come on, don't start with the waterworks."

I aggressively swiped the traitorous tears from my cheeks, rage sweeping through me like a tsunami. I was Alicia motherfucking Thorne, and I would not wallow beneath the heels of an insecure, emotionally stunted twenty-nine-year-old man-child.

So, when I opened my mouth, I let all that built-up frustration sore forth to hit him square in the chest as his words played on repeat inside my head.

Next, you're going to tell me how much you've fallen in love with me, right? How you can't live without me? How I will never find another woman like you?

"Yes, Ethan. Over the past four years, I have fallen in love with you, and congratulations, you've successfully spat on that in the timespan of a few minutes. But let me clarify a few things for you, *famous football player*, since you've seemed to get a few things twisted. First, I *can* and *will* live without you."

When I mentioned that pesky four-letter L word, I thought he was having a coronary from the way his eyes were bulging. But I didn't let him get a word in. Grabbing his shoulders, I pushed him fully out the door and out of my apartment.

"When I said I wanted a partner, a husband, a father for my kids, I didn't mean you. Oh, yeah, I was *hoping* you would be willing to explore all those possibilities with me, share in that future. But make no mistake, I can have all those things *without you.*"

Ethan tried to step forward, but I didn't let him, shoving him back an extra step. He managed to right his stance and straighten to his full height, giving me his severe stare. By his expression alone, I was glad he was now outside, in the corridor. He was livid—absolutely seething. I could tell he was gearing up to give me *all* the words and unload on me.

Nope. Not going to happen. I don't want to hear all his toxic mummy issues bullshit... not again.

So before he could spit his venom, I cut him off once more. "Out of all of those warped lies you've told yourself, Ethan. I will give you one concession. There is one fact that you managed to get right—you will *never* find another woman like me."

Then, I slammed the door in his shocked, stupid face.

Strike one.

Chapter 2

ALICIA

Bad things come in threes. That's the superstition, right?

I didn't know if I could handle one more.

For the first time in my life, I told a partner, *"I love you"*. I didn't know how it was supposed to feel after, but I didn't think it was supposed to feel like my heart was beating out of rhythm.

After that disastrous conversation with Ethan, I had gone no contact when he left for his away game.

Yet, he still managed to send me his regular pregame text as if he hadn't just insulted me in every possible way.

> Wish me luck, love. Looking forward to reading your commentary after the game.

I scoffed. *Is he for real?* Yes. Yes, he was. The arrogant bastard.

We had come up with our own unofficial ritual over the years. Ethan would text me before he hit the field. I would send him a string of messages throughout the game—mostly of ridiculous observations—and he would read them after, which he swore helped him unwind and decompress from all the adrenalin, bringing him back down to earth. Seeing the game from the perspective of someone who didn't exactly enjoy football apparently made my take on things *hilarious*.

Not anymore. After his insults, I didn't even bother watching him play. Why would I? I only ever watched it for him. And Ethan didn't deserve my sharp humour and winning personality.

However, my ignoring him pissed him right off based on his follow-up texts that night, which became increasingly demanding as time progressed.

Are you really sulking right now?

God, I thought that after our conversation, you would get over yourself.

Why didn't you watch me play?

You've never ignored me before. Where are you, Ali?

ALICIA!!

And after several missed calls?

ANSWER YOUR PHONE!

I would have laughed at his blatant desperation, except I was interrupted by a different call. One that every person dreaded.

Strike two hit me with the brute force of a battering ram, dropping me to my knees.

Phil Thorne, my solid rock of a dad, had had a stroke.

I was still reeling from my mother's sobs over the phone as she called her daughters back to Acacia Falls—the small town we spent most of our teenage years. I kept on zoning out in the passenger seat as my older sister, Alexis, sped down the highway leading us out of the city.

It was the middle of the night. Austin, my three-year-old nephew, slept in the backseat as my sister and I talked in circles.

When we finally arrived at the hospital hours later, Dad's condition had thankfully stabilised. He still had a long way to go, but we were so relieved to know he wasn't in immediate danger.

We all made camp in his hospital room, waiting for sunrise, not wanting to leave in case he or Mum needed anything.

For the first time in hours, I was able to breathe. I settled back in an uncomfortable recliner shoved in the corner, slipped on my headphones and doom scrolled online, looking for any distraction to calm my mind.

That's when strike three came barrelling toward me at full speed, threatening to total me to the ground without any fucking padding whatsoever.

The viral video was taken from an odd angle, the person behind the camera was inconspicuous but in the perfect position to get a clear shot of Ethan.

He stood tall and proud in the middle of a crowded bar, surrounded by a couple of football buddies and countless party girls. With quite a few drinks under his belt and an enraptured audience, Ethan's bolstered speech carried above them all.

"This chick wants me to marry her. She's delusional. In all these years, I haven't even acknowledged her in public," he claimed with a proud expression.

He can't possibly be talking about... me?

"What if she tries to baby-trap you?" Jake asked. He was known as one of the looser cannon players on the football team, always getting into trouble.

Ethan sneered. "She won't. She's a good girl who listens to everything I say."

A beautiful woman saddled up to his side, skating a suggestive hand down his arm. "That doesn't sound like fun." She even managed to tack on a pout at the end.

"Hmm, you may be right, darlin'."

"Then why do you go back?" Jake asked, digging for more, egging him on to speak absolute trash.

"It's not me who comes back. It's just *easy*, Jakey boy. No commitments means no demands and no expectations. I get *whatever* I want, *whenever* I want." His suggestive tone implied exactly what "whatever" meant.

"Hmm, I dunno. I'm not convinced. You've been seeing this mystery woman for a long time, bro."

"And what? You've never met her, right? When I tell you this girl isn't even marriage material, let alone mother material... " His speech tapered off as he took a long drag from his beer while the surrounding females cackled in laughter.

His eyes spread over the crowd, his satisfied expression deepening from the enthusiastic reception. Ethan looked and spoke as if he were a king holding court amongst his subjects.

"Although, the usual does get a bit stale after a while," he continued, his gaze catching on the woman who still hadn't removed her claws from his fucking arm. "I probably won't be able to resist much longer."

The woman preened while Jake gave a mocking scoff. "I'll believe it when I see it."

"Is that a challenge?" Ethan asked with intoxicated and affronted eyes.

Jake's lips twisted into a cruel smirk. "Yeah, maybe it is."

Without a beat of hesitation, Ethan drew the woman next to him into his chest and pressed his mouth to hers, their tongues dancing together in a disgusting display of saliva.

That's when the video cut out.

I was encapsulated in a quiet hospital room with my family, soft snores occasionally breaking through the deafening silence.

But all I could hear was an internal scream rebounding in my skull, a never-ending screech that refused to abate with the realisation of Ethan's words and actions, sinking deep and true.

The video was only a few minutes long, but that was all it took for maximum damage to be spread.

I opened Ethan's text thread and found a few unread messages from earlier in the night before his nauseating performance was broadcast all over the internet.

Alright, I get it. I'll give you some space then come and see you when I'm back.

I was just shocked, love. You know I'm not good at that stuff. We will talk soon.

Miss you.

What a fucking joke.

***Or** am **I** the joke?*

I felt like a fool. Taken for granted. Absolutely *humiliated.*

Of course, over the past four years, I had made a rookie error and fell in love with *the* famous running back, Ethan Harris. But when I laid those revelations on him, I at least expected to walk away as friends—at the very least.

But whoever the person in that video was... I didn't know him. That person was cruel and vicious, not at all *my* Ethan—someone I had grown to respect and know.

Whoever that was... they weren't worth knowing at all.

I blocked him.

Chapter 3

ETHAN

I woke with a groggy start, my mouth parched and my head pounding with a violent hangover. Geez, I didn't even know what time I got home.

I swiped my phone from the nightstand, the screen laden with notifications. It was the usual sight, but even so, the sheer amount was way more than usual.

Right then, a message beeped through from Jake.

Bro, you've gone viral. Fucking hilarious.

I rubbed my eyes, letting them adjust out of my half-asleep stupor, then clicked on the link he had sent.

One minute turned into two as dread filtered through my system as the video played. By the end of the clip, I was fully awake. By then, I didn't know if I had a headache as an aftereffect of all the alcohol or from the self-loathing I garnered from watching myself act a fool.

I trash-talked Alicia. *My* Alicia. All for my overinflated ego.

What made it even worse? I kissed some random groupie. Sure, it hadn't gone any further, but the video definitely didn't suggest that. It cut out at the most inopportune moment, ending with that disgusting kiss that appeared to be a lot more than what it was.

Vomit-inducing was what it *actually* was. Figuratively and literally. After that messy lip-lock, I got so sick I ran for the toilets to upend my guts. Soon after, Jake dragged me home, laughing at me all the way.

I didn't even know why I let him convince me to go out. We weren't that tight, but what was worse was that I let him bait me into acting like a fucking teenager, preening for attention.

Unable to resist, I poured over the page that had posted the incriminating footage. It belonged to some popular influencer named Katy, who happened to be in the same bar at the exact right time. She claimed she was doing the people's work by exposing my disgusting behaviour. She found me abhorrent. *Get in line.*

The video had already gained one million views, and it hadn't even been twenty-four hours. Taking full advantage of the traction, Katy already followed up with another video, giving her added commentary on the whole scene.

Fucking great. Of course, I clicked on it.

"...Ethan Harris, everybody. What a douchebag. If anything, I feel sorry for the girl he mentioned. He obviously has no respect for her, and if she had any respect for herself, she would leave his stupid..."

I zoned out her tirade, flipping to the comments. The hashtag #runawaygirl was trending all over, which had my gut churning—again.

The world had declared me public enemy number one, the masses calling for me to be cancelled. If only I gave a shit about that.

All I cared about was my girl. *Has she seen this? Of course she's fucking seen this!*

Fear had me opening Alicia's contact. I called her number—and it bounced.

What the fuck?

I tried again… and again. Nothing. *Fuck this.* Typing out in rapid sequence, I sent whatever came to mind, firing off message after message.

I didn't mean what I said.

I was drunk.

That kiss didn't mean anything.

It made me sick.

When I was in the middle of typing out the next, I realised a bright red sign flashed beneath each text. *Not delivered.* Which was the only thing I was grateful for that morning. As I reread each statement, my shame grew exponentially. Fuck. Even to me, it sounded like a load of shit.

Before I could ruminate further, my phone rang, and I answered my dad's call on autopilot. I shouldn't have.

"My boy, what is going on!? I went fishing with Ralph this morning, and he showed me some video. A disturbing video. Tell me it isn't you," he said in a rush.

I sighed. "*Dad.*"

That's all it took. That one word, said in such a guilty tone that it completely set him off.

"How could you, Ethan? I did not raise you to say such cruel things. I swore to Ralph that wasn't my boy in the video. I insisted that my son would *never* speak about anyone like that, let alone a woman that he had been seeing for—what was it? Years?"

His disappointment rang true. Rudy Harris was a formidable man who raised me as a single father. He was my guiding light, and I respected him above all else. There was only one other who had ever come close to that type of calibre and meaning in my life... and I had just reduced her to the dirt beneath my feet for all the whole world to see.

Dad continued to berate me. "...is this the girl that you've mentioned before? The one you wanted me to meet next time I came to visit?"

I gave a sharp grunt—the only confirmation I'd allow. I didn't trust my emotions enough to speak out loud, not knowing what would come out.

"Why would you say such horrible things about her, Ethan? Why would you embarrass her and kiss some nobody? What happened with your Alicia?"

"Dad!" I interrupted. *Your Alicia.* Hearing the name I had claimed as mine... God, I couldn't take it anymore. Everything culminated in that tragic moment where I was on the precipice of losing it all.

I cleared my throat. "Dad, *I fucked up*."

"Oh, son, you really have."

Chapter 4

ALICIA

It was late in the evening, my parents' house quiet as I sank into bed, exhausted and emotionally drained after one hell of a week.

All our focus remained on Dad and his recovery. I was thankful for my ex-brother-in-law, Owen, who was assigned as his physiotherapist.

I used to consider him as close as a brother. Until he cheated on my sister with one of her close friends. If that wasn't bad enough, he managed to knock the bitch up.

Over four years had passed, and I could still see the residual pain in my sister's eyes when he was near. I could also see the longing... From both sides.

Despite their history, however, Dad seemed to trust Owen's word, which helped kick his old stubborn pride into gear. We also respected Alexis' opinion, being a nurse. She was able to bridge our diverse levels of understanding and keep everyone informed and in the loop.

But that didn't stop normal life from moving on.

My boss, Felix Johnson, had called me earlier that afternoon, wanting to discuss a high-level contract I had been negotiating for one of my clients. It was a big case, and one I had been preparing and working on for two months straight. The level of complexity the contract required meant it had the potential to catapult me to the prestigious position of Executive Financial Advisor—a role I had worked my ass off to achieve. And with that contract, I was truly on the cusp of moving higher professionally.

Although Felix was cutthroat and expected perfection from his employees, he was also severely family-orientated, as proven by his naming his entire company after his wife. So, due to my circumstances, he immediately reassured me and let me know he would take over my case if needed.

Except I didn't give him an answer, requesting a little more time to think. My family needed me; my *Dad* needed me. But I couldn't bring myself to fully let go of the opportunity, which made guilt eat away at my conscience. It was difficult to accept, to hand all my hard work over for someone else to reap the rewards.

So I gave myself a night. One night. To wallow in self-pity, lick my wounds and come to terms with my new reality.

I lost my man—who wasn't even my man to begin with. I lost my pride. And now, I was about to lose my big contract at work.

Fuck my fucking life.

Silent tears began to run down my face until they turned into a torrent of sobs that soon became uncontrollable. I tried to keep my emotions locked up, so I didn't disturb my sister or nephew sleeping down the hall.

It didn't work. I felt the mattress dip before warm arms wrapped me up tight from behind. Which only made me sob harder.

Alexis remained calm, stroking my hair as she repeated, "I'm here."

With the soothing presence of my sister, my tongue soon loosened, unloading my pathetic existence for her to weigh and judge.

Alexis surprised me.

She blamed herself for not being there for me. *Preposterous.*

She even offered to help hide the body of a certain man... a very handsome, charismatic traitor of a man. *Okay, not so preposterous.*

We continued to talk into the night, a sense of peace settling over us both as we shared our thoughts like so many times before. That I decided to unburden myself with my last remaining reservation. "It's been a week, and my work has been calling, asking for a return date."

Alexis had an idea of the case I was working on since I had confided in her throughout.

"What do you want to do?" she asked.

Familiar guilt slashed through me. "Dad... I can't leave him."

"Yes, you can." I turned on my side, her silhouette sharpening with her words. "I will move back temporarily with Austin. Having him around will help with Dad's recovery while also keeping Mum busy."

I sighed. "Alexis, you don't have to—"

"I want to." She cut me off. "You know I've been contemplating moving Austin out of the city for a while. I can also help Dad if I stay here with them, use my presence as an excuse to bully him into listening to the doctors instead of ignoring them."

I fell quiet, letting what she said sink in. *Was it fair to leave her behind in this?* Then Alexis bulldozed through my reservations with her own concerns.

"Will you be okay though, Ali? Going back there, I mean... If you see him?" she asked. "I don't want you to be alone if that happens."

Bitterness rushed forth at the mere mention of *him*.

I may have been using my family crisis as a distraction to not think about that video. Or, more specifically, the main person highlighted in that video.

Even so, the reminder would always hit me unawares. When I paused to take a breather or when I had a spare minute of the day. My thoughts would always unintentionally sway back to that two-minute window where my character was entirely destroyed on screen.

Yeah, his scathing words hurt. But that was nothing compared to the humiliation. Some person even ranted online about how I should respect myself, going so far as to start a hashtag #runawaygirl. The whole internet saw him reject me and felt *sorry* for me... And that just made me fucking *livid.*

"*Fuck him*. He will not run me out just because of *his* fucked up actions. I have nothing to be ashamed of. And, oh"—I clicked on my phone to check the incriminating clip again—"three million random people on the internet agree with me so far." *Geez, three million and counting.* The only consolation was knowing that he was getting absolutely roasted online. *Good. Wallow in despair, asshole.*

Chapter 5

ETHAN

I raced over to Alicia's apartment as soon as I knew she had arrived back in the city. It had been just over a week since my life imploded, and I'd heard no word from her. Not even a damn smoke signal.

How irresponsible! I needed to know if she was safe and staying off the internet.

As someone always in the limelight, I knew how cruel people could be—proven by everyone who was currently hunting me down with pitchforks. Sure, it didn't make me feel all warm and fuzzy inside, but I didn't give a fuck. I was only concerned for Alicia.

I thought of the messages I had sent earlier that fateful night. The ones that actually went through.

> Alright, I get it. I'll give you some space then come and see you when I'm back.

Straight after I had found out about the video and received the worst verbal lashing from my Dad. I booked the first flight home.

All calls to Alicia bounced, which I accepted. What I didn't expect was to find her apartment empty when I arrived.

I was just shocked, love. You know I'm not good at that stuff. We will talk soon.

I told her we would talk soon, so why the fuck did she run off before we could even discuss anything?

Miss you.

That last message hit different—a minute tell of my vulnerability at the time. It had me reeling with anxiety—and, dare I say it, nerves. I wasn't used to expressing those types of emotions, didn't like being victim of them.

After my disastrous reaction in her apartment, freshly followed up my foolish drunken rants, I knew I was fucked.

I had to see her. To apologise and try to explain why I had reacted the way I did.

But more importantly, I had to communicate why I was as messed up as I was. My issues ran deep, and when she had dropped those commitment bombs on me, I panicked. It had me reverting back to my childhood days when I would have to switch from defence to offence in a manner of seconds.

I had to make Alicia understand that, although my actions showed it was everything to do with her. It, in fact, had everything to do with *me*.

Seeing her was the only thing that was going to relieve the weird ache that had taken root inside me.

So, as soon as I made it back to the city, I sat in the foyer of Alicia's apartment building for hours, waiting for her to come home. I didn't know how much time passed until the same doorman returned for his next shift, finding me in the exact position I was in before he had left.

The older gentleman approached with sincere eyes, his name badge flashing on his chest. "Son, have you had something to eat?" Burt asked.

I shook my head.

"Sleep?"

I repeated the motion, scared to talk in case I screamed instead.

"Who is it you're waiting for?"

I licked my dry lips. "Alicia. She's on level sixteen. Reception said they can't get a hold of anyone in the apartment, and she... she broke her phone, so I can't get in touch with her."

Burt's face softened. "Ah, Miss Thorne." My attention spiked at the mention of her name. "She may be away. She does work hard, that girl."

Work. Idiot!

"You're a damn genius, Burt."

Seeming pleased with my reaction, Burt returned to his station near the entrance as I called Alicia's office at Stella Financial Management.

I immediately deflated as Felix, her boss, answered. Clearing my throat, I managed to ask for Alicia.

"Sorry, Mr Harris, but Miss Thorne has taken some emergency leave. I'm currently looking after her clients. What can I help you with?"

Emergency leave? Alicia worked fast and didn't fuck around, as proven by her swift escape. *Runaway girl, indeed.*

Things were more dire than I had realised.

"Ah, nothing. Can you get her to call me when she's available?"

"Of course. Are you sure I can't—"

"Nope." Then I hung up. It was probably a dick move. *Which was the norm for me now.*

I found myself pacing, unsure of what my next play should be. *Who else could I use to get in contact with her?*

I hadn't even met any of her family or friends. *What is wrong with me?*

We would usually hook up at my place, but on occasion, I would go to her apartment when her sister and nephew weren't there. Alicia never offered or asked for me to meet them, but I also never showed interest in that part of her life.

Hence, I had nowhere else to turn. No clues to follow. Further proving how much of a self-absorbed asshole I was.

As I shuffled past Burt, he laid a hand on my shoulder, which sent a spark to my brain. Before I could talk myself out of it, I hit him with an offer that we both couldn't refuse.

"Burt, if you message me when Miss Thorne returns, I will pay you $20,000."

He narrowed his eyes. Professional façade gone. "She's a good girl. I'm not letting you or any man loose on her."

A spark of respect registered. But that didn't help my situation. "I'm good for the money, if that's what you're worried about?"

"I'm not going to let you hurt her," he said, his voice hard as steel.

I huffed. "If anything, I'll be the one who gets hurt." *When she slaps me upside the head.* "I won't even touch her."

"There are other ways to hurt someone, Mr Harris."

Awareness and disappointment flashed in the older man's eyes, causing shame to ignite in mine. He had known who I was the whole time.

"Now, how about we make a deal," he continued as if he didn't just gut me on the spot. "You will give me $50,000 in return for one text. *But* I come with you. You do not enter her apartment. You do not touch her. You do not threaten her in any way. I will be there... watching."

Man, who does he think I am, some stalker?

Well, he'd have a point there.

"I swear. I only want to talk to her."

He assessed me a minute longer, then offered a hard handshake. "We've struck a deal."

"Deal."

I had waited and waited for that pesky text to come through for days, wondering if I had been conned by the innocent-looking doorman called Burt. I had only sent him half the money as insurance, but after no word, I was definitely contemplating my life choices.

Until my phone beeped, and I was in the car and on the road in sixty seconds flat.

I gave myself a pep talk on the way to her apartment. Rallying towards my next play.

I'll let her yell, scream, cuss me out—anything. Probably even consider letting her throw hands and land a few, too.

We were both fiery and hot-headed—that's what originally attracted us to one another. Alicia was extremely passionate, and I didn't hold back either, which usually converted to the best outcome in the bedroom. We were a burning inferno together in nature and personality, yet that often spilled over in overzealous words or regretful disputes.

As proven by Subject A—me. This time, I didn't know if a weak apology would be enough... The thought had me terrified.

I didn't even remember driving all the way to her apartment complex, but the next thing I processed was barging into the elevator with Burt chasing behind.

"Breathe," he said from behind my shoulder, the reminder well-taken as I followed his command.

When the elevator slid open, I took one more deep breath, made my way to Alicia's door and knocked.

I was ready for her rage. *Come at me, love. Burn me up and spit me out. Just give me another chance.*

After the longest five minutes known to mankind, the front door swung open, giving me the first glimpse of her in what felt like forever.

But what I found wasn't what I expected.

I anticipated my fiery little vixen spitting insults and curses my way. But there was none.

Instead, there stood Alicia. Stone-cold, apathetic and utterly indifferent. As if I didn't matter. As if *we* didn't matter... As if I were a stranger.

Chapter 6

ALICIA

I gave him my girl-boss face. My take-no-shit, kick-ass, business face. Even though my eyes wanted to roam down his body, to catalogue where I'd lay my hands to pull him closer.

No. Have some dignity, woman.

Ethan stood frozen before me as if he had been knocked off balance. *Good.* Taking advantage of the reprieve, I rolled my shoulders back and folded my arms, waiting for his grand speech.

"I'm sorry," he blurted. His demeanour calmed immediately post as if he had unloaded some huge revelation. For him, I was sure it was since that was probably the first time he had ever apologised... to anyone.

Silence fell heavily between us as I refused to budge.

Was that it? His remorse was laughable at best. I pitched a sarcastic brow, prepared to wait him out.

Ethan cleared his throat and his dumbstruck expression, finally collecting himself.

"Can I come in?"

"Nope."

"Did you see the video?"

"Yep."

"Are you only going to give me one-word answers?"

"Maybe."

I could see his features spasming from my monotone responses. Despite everything that Ethan said, he had miscalculated one vital piece of information. I *knew* him.

After being intimate with someone for four years, it's hard not to learn all their tells, the subtle nuances that made them tick.

And Ethan... By his tone and expression alone, I could tell he was getting frustrated. This was new territory for us. He expected a reaction out of me, which I wasn't going to give him. Ethan deserved nothing, so I gave him nothing.

"Where have you been?" he said, his tone on the verge of rudeness.

"None of your business."

"Can you give me more words and actually talk to me?"

"I just gave you four," I said with a confused frown.

Ethan ran a hand through his hair in irritation. *That's right, boo, get angry.* "Alicia... That video..."

"I don't care about the video," I said with a straight face, although my insides shrivelled up at the blatant lie—but I powered through. "Ethan, if that's how you felt about me, you should have ended things ages ago."

A stagnant pause stretched forth as he processed my uncaring front. Ethan had never seen me so passive, and for once in his life, he didn't know what to do.

"That's not how I feel, love."

"Well, all evidence to the contrary."

"Alicia, I came here to tell you—"

"I think I've heard all I want to hear of what you have to say on the subject, actually, thanks. I'm done now."

Ethan flinched as if I'd just slapped him—he would have deserved it if I had.

"Well. I guess that's it, then?" He phrased it as a question, putting out feelers for any change around. Ethan was probably expecting me to beg him to stay or something. *Never.*

"Yep. That's it."

I could see his eye twitching as he shifted to leave. "I'm going now."

"Bye." I even managed a finger wave.

"I guess I don't have to feel guilty anymore..."

That jackass.

"I absolve you of any guilt. You don't need to have any on my behalf since I don't feel anything for you anymore. We're done."

Ethan practically malfunctioned before me, his panicked eyes cataloguing my professional, plastic smile.

"Done?"

"Yes. That's what you wanted, no?"

"Ali, about what I said—"

"—Hmm, I don't have all night to unpack *everything* you said, Ethan. I've already wasted enough time on you."

"Stop acting like this," he snapped.

"Like what?"

"Like you don't care. *I know you do,*" he said, desperation seeping into the edges of his voice.

With an eerily straight face, I decided to strike the match and light the fucking fuse. "But Ethan, I *don't* care."

Boom!

"You could have fooled me, Alicia! You ran away for a whole fucking week because you *cared* so much. Emergency leave? Yeah, I looked you up. You're not as unfazed as you're making yourself out to be. Now, let me in so we can sort this shit out."

The problem with igniting an explosive was the unpredictable shattering effect. I had every intention of blowing him up, but I had unintentionally been caught in the crossfire.

Emergency leave? *My Dad had a fucking stroke!*

My unrelenting mask seemed to crack around the seams as I lost all rational thought, leaving only anger roaring behind.

Retreating a few steps to my console table, I collected the last gift he had bought me, then proceeded to beat him with it.

"Ah! Fuck! Stop!" Ethan yelled, his arms raised to protect himself from the pink dildo repeatedly launching for his face.

After one final whack, I chucked the toy at his chest. "Now, go and fuck yourself!" I screamed, then slammed the door in his stupid, shocked face.

Barely breathing, I spied through the peephole and watched Ethan silently implode behind the door. My lovely neighbours came to check if everything was alright, and I nearly fucking died when they asked for an autograph as he tried to disguise the dildo beneath his shirt.

The sight had me so close to squealing, but I smothered that bitch down by holding a firm hand over my mouth.

When Ethan finished his celebrity obligations, he went to bang on my door again until Burt laid a hand on his shoulder, whispering something in his ear. After a long minute, Burt managed to steer Ethan towards the elevator.

The showdown I had been dreading actually turned out a lot better than I had expected. I bid him goodbye—even said we were done. That was our four years put to rest with nil room to move forward. It was over, and now, I would surely be able to forget him and move on... right?

I turned for the kitchen, in desperate need of wine, when a knock rang through. After checking, I opened the door to my adorable, middle-aged doorman.

"Thanks for the heads up, Burt. Now, make sure he sends you the other half of the money."

Burt had messaged me immediately following Ethan's proposition, asking what I wanted to do. Of course, I couldn't resist the opportunity.

"But... ah. I was actually going to return the money, Miss Thorne."

"Why would you do that?"

"Well, you said you had a few things to say to him. Now that it's done, I thought the ruse was over."

"Oh, Burt. There is no ruse. You had an arrangement, and you kept to your part. He will too. Keep the money... for Imogen."

His wife was sick—the type of sick that didn't get better. He could use the extra funds—deserved them, actually.

Although Burt had a hard time accepting it. "But—"

"No buts. Ethan made that deal. Let him live up to it."

He looked dazed but gave a shallow nod. "Um... I better get back to work." I smiled, and his expression softened. "I'm proud of you, kid."

"Oh, my dear Burt, I wish I could say the same. $50,000 for leverage on *me*? You should have asked for $100,000," I said with a wink before closing the door.

Burt's deep chuckle lingered behind, giving way to my own.

Chapter 7

ETHAN

I didn't even make it through the front door, having it out in the communal hallway so her neighbours could eavesdrop and catch me in the most perilous position—with a fucking pink dildo shoved halfway up my shirt and a killer bruise forming on my cheekbone.

Fucking hell. My girl had a mean right hook... especially with a solid weapon in her hand.

I wasn't fazed about her outburst. If anything, I was glad when she finally snapped and showed me some of that emotion—even if it did involve Alicia knocking some sense into me. *Who knew a plastic dick could be more useful than my actual dick? Not me.*

Sure, I was an immature fool for baiting her, but I was disturbed, entirely unhinged when faced with Alicia's cold indifference. I was dealing with a new woman. Someone I hadn't met before.

I went there with the intention of saying so much, but instead, I lost my composure and spewed pure shit instead.

I fumbled... *again*. And I had no fucking idea how to pull myself out of the gigantic hole I had trapped myself in.

Alicia said we were done, which I was unable to accept. I had to keep fighting, invading her space to show Alicia that *she* was what I wanted.

And that's what I intended to do.

Buckle up, love. I'm coming for you.

Alicia still had me blocked, so I tried the only form of contact I had access to.

A few dial tones rang when she answered the phone. "Stella Financial Management, Alicia speaking."

"Ali, it's Ethan."

"Who?"

"You heard me, love. I need to see you."

Beep. Beep. Beep. She hung up on me.

I didn't even hesitate to press redial. When she answered again, her professional cadence had a bit of flint to it.

"I'm not sure who this is, but if you don't stop harassing me, I'll have security block your calls."

Beep. Beep. Beep.

She wouldn't even let me get a word in. Lucky for her, I was just giving a courtesy call since I was already on my way.

I lied to the front desk and said I had an appointment with Alicia, and Felix's secretary was too busy eye-fucking me to actually check the schedule properly.

Alicia's office was down a secluded corridor, and I was lucky enough not to run into anyone along the way, which could only mean that my impromptu visit was meant to be.

As I approached closer, I found the door ajar as two female voices carried through.

"Have you got everything packed?" Alicia asked.

"Pretty much. This should be our last trip for a while. You sure you're going to be okay on your own? I know you didn't want to come back and leave him," said the stranger's voice.

Him? Who the fuck is him*?*

"Of course, Lex. Don't worry about me. Pour all that energy into Dad," Alicia replied, then her voice dipped. "How is he doing?"

My foot faltered, instinct warning me to take a step back. I had never heard her so vulnerable. She was having a private conversation with Lex—her *sister*,Alexis.

"He's doing surprisingly well—don't give me that look, Ali. I mean it. For someone who has just had a stroke, he's doing better than expected..."

The rest of their conversation filtered off as I processed the monumental news that I had fallen upon. More accurately, eavesdropped on.

I shouldn't be here. I should not fucking be here, listening to this.

My insides were warring in existential crisis—cataloguing all the bullshit I had thrown at Alicia since she had confessed her feelings for me.

Her father had a bloody stroke, and I was so self-absorbed that I blamed her for running from me.

Oh, no. I had to get out of there.

I stumbled backward, about to retreat, but of course, fate decided to shit on me further, preventing my escape.

Alexis exited the office with a young boy tethered to her hand. She hadn't spotted me yet, closing the door behind her.

They looked exactly like their family portraits hanging in Alicia's apartment. A weird sensation took me over as their stationary smiles shifted to real life before my eyes.

Then she turned, her frame immediately seizing when her green orbs caught on me. Her bitter gaze made me cold, as if my brain was getting freezer burn the longer I remained in her presence.

"Um, nice to meet you," I croaked.

"Hmm, is it?"

Why did I engage? It wasn't a conscious thought—my mind was in survival mode, so my mouth was running on its own.

Shut your fucking mouth, idiot.

I pivoted my gaze from her narrowed one to the young boy beside her, searching for some reprieve from her unimpressed glare.

The little guy tilted his head, perusing me with open curiosity. *That's it!*

I gave him my most charming, gleaming smile—the one I gave all my fans and decided would win over Alicia's nephew.

"You want an autograph, young fella?"

"What's an autograph?"

Umm, awkward. Metaphorical crickets sounded between us. *Fucking kill me. Dead. Right now, please.*

"Ahh, it's a signature. My name for you to keep later, to show you met me."

"Why? Who are you?"

Alexis smirked. "Yeah, who are you?"

I cringed. The animosity flowing from Alexis was suffocating. There was no doubt she knew who I was—especially who I was to Alicia.

"Mama, is he my daddy?"

What the fuck? Do all kids just go around asking this stuff?

I blanched while Alexis scoffed. "No, Austin. I wouldn't call this man *husband* material, let alone *father* material."

Oof. Nothing worse than someone quoting your biggest regret back at you.

Alexis steered Austin around me, making for the exit before giving me her parting blow.

"We won't waste your time any further. We're going to have to *run away* now."

Checkmate and done. Outplayed and outmanoeuvred by another Thorne.

I was done.

Chapter 8

ALICIA

I slumped back in my office chair, my eyes lapsing shut as I massaged my temples—a sorry attempt to get rid of the headache that just wouldn't quit.

I distantly processed the door clicking open and closed as someone slipped inside. *Alexis must have forgotten something.*

"Alicia..."

That voice. I knew that voice. But I had never heard it in that tone before. Pained, hesitant... vulnerable.

I refused to open my eyes, refused to engage in another standoff. I didn't have the energy.

"I can't do this right now. *I'm tired.*" I could have sworn I had aged a decade over the past month alone.

"Ali, please look at me," Ethan said. *Was that a little sniffle I heard in there? Good. Choke on it.* "Please, love. Give me those eyes."

My lids cracked a sliver, and what I saw nearly made me gasp. Ethan sat across my desk in what I could only call a submissive stance. Hunched shoulders, head bowed with a doe-eyed expression.

What the hell happened to Ethan Harris?

"Alicia, I need to apologise."

"For what?"

"Fuck, where do I even start?" Ethan's stare penetrated, blue eyes blazing with emotion as his hands opened in sincerity. "There's an endless list, but let's start from the beginning."

"*I'm so sorry, Alicia.* For the way I initially reacted to your feelings, for being so condescending and uncaring. For my immaturity, blowing up your phone. And that video—*god*, how I wish I could just erase that night. Better yet, erase everything after you tried having that talk with me... I would change so much..."

For the first time ever, he was completely open, allowing me to see right into the depths of him. If only that could erase the bitterness he had injected into my bloodstream. Guarding against further hurt, I remained silent and fortified my apathetic persona.

Ethan sighed. "Those things I said about you were disgusting, straight-up lies. I have never felt that way about you, *ever*. You weren't just a fuck buddy to me, Ali. Over the years, you have steadily become my best friend, and I can't believe I let my weak ego take over and treat you the way I did...

"Then I had to fuck myself further and cheat on you. We promised exclusivity, and I managed to shit on our arrangement, our friendship, our connection for a vomit-inducing kiss. I swear it didn't go further than that, but that doesn't excuse anything. My actions were deplorable, and when you immediately shut me out, I didn't know how to cope. I was a fucking toddler chucking a tantrum over not having your attention, not having your light shining on me any longer."

Confusion was steadily building as Ethan gave me his grand apology speech. I was sceptical at best, his turnaround making me question our entire history and him as a person.

I tilted my head, taking him in. "Are you... feeling, okay? Have you been diagnosed with anything recently?"

His brow furrowed. "No. Why?"

"Because your behaviour and mood swings are giving me whiplash. First, your arrogance was so potent. That shit was infectious—as proven by your little groupies cackling in that video. Now, you're practically on your knees. For what? What happened to the pro football player who was a king amongst men?"

"I'm no king without my queen. And Ali, I want—"

I scoffed. "Yes, let's start there. What do you want this time, *Superstar*? You already crushed my heart, now you want my liver too?"

Ethan's hair was a mess, his anxious hands pulling on the strands while exhaustion slowly pulled me down further. I was running on fumes and didn't have anything extra to spare for this crap.

"Look, Ethan. I acknowledge the apology, but it doesn't change anything. I have a lot going on, and let me just say you're the last thing on my priority list. Better yet, you're not even on the list. Work and family are what's important to me right now."

Ethan's head bobbled as sympathy painted his features. "Ali. Your dad. *Fuck*, I'm so sorry, love. I want to help. Tell me what I can do."

"*Leave me alone.*"

Chapter 9

ALICIA

"L*eave me alone.*"

Tears gathered in my lash line as the monumental request took root. I meant them, and Ethan knew it. I didn't know how he found out about my dad, but it didn't matter.

Be strong, Alicia.

"That's not something I can give you, love," he said, voice soft, almost lost.

Minutes ticked by as his face gradually morphed into a resolute mask. "I'm not going anywhere. I lost sight of us for a second, but I'm going to make amends. And I'll start by paying for your dad's medical expenses."

My eyes snapped with fire, that previous sadness completely evaporated, replaced with frustration.

He could hear me, but he wasn't fucking processing a word.

I sliced a hand through the air. "And here he is, folks. I don't want your guilt money, Ethan."

"I'm only trying to—"

"When are you going to get it? Not everything can be solved with money, power or influence."

"But... but you've been accepting my gifts," he said, having the audacity to sound disappointed.

"Why would I waste completely good merchandise? Those donuts are delicious, the flowers are beautiful, and the lingerie is my favourite brand. I took those gifts because I fucking deserve them! That doesn't mean we're getting back together."

Ethan was shaking. "Then I'll buy you more shit. We can go public. No secrets this time. Anything you want, Ali. Whatever you want."

A potent dejection slowly took hold. We were on two separate wavelengths that kept on missing the reconnect.

"That's not what I want, Ethan. That's never what I wanted. Your money, status, going public? None of that mattered to me."

"Then *tell* me what you want."

"There's no point. 'Cause no matter what I say, you won't actually *listen*." I shook my head. "What's that saying? *When someone shows you who they are, believe them.* Well, trust me, *Mr Harris*, I was watching—alongside the whole world—and I received your message loud and clear. No misinterpretation on my part. I believed you wholeheartedly."

"That's not who I am. You *know* me. Please, Alicia, you are one of the very few people who really knows me."

"I thought I did... but as soon as I asked the hard questions, laid those commitments on you, you turned cruel. The attentive, gorgeous man I knew disappeared right before my eyes. As if he never existed at all. Instead, he was body-snatched, his personality swapped out by a pubescent fuck boy that searched for validation from strangers. People who don't give a fuck about him."

Ethan's head bowed low. If he lowered any further, his forehead would hit the floor. "The man you've been with for the past four years. The man you fell in love with. That's the *real* me."

"Loved."

"Huh?"

"Loved—as in past tense."

Ethan shuddered as if he were struck with a live electrical wire, devastation coating his features. "I will earn back your affection, Ali. I'll earn back your love. I'm going to prove myself to you."

A pretty speech with pretty words. I also took note that he never professed any such feelings for me. *So why the fuck is he here?*

I sighed. "Show me some respect."

"You're one of the very few people in my life I do respect, Ali."

"Your actions don't align with your words. What you did isn't respectful. The way you've treated me isn't respectful. You being here *at my job*, trying to bulldoze me into getting what you want is not respectful!"

Stella Financial Management had a strict, ironclad, no fraternisation policy. Due to the calibre of clients, there were a lot of social climbers who wanted a spot in the industry—to get close to the rich and famous. I was not going to give up my job for a man.

So, Ethan coming into my workplace, wanting to discuss our personal issues—more like bully me into forgiveness—caused a volcano of rage to erupt inside me.

"It's over, Ethan. Leave. Now."

Red raised up his neck, and his eyes swam with a certain type of unhinged quality. He was about to blow, and I was not fucking having it.

He went to stand, and my hand automatically curled over the photo frame on my desk. The dildo obviously wasn't enough to beat some common decency into him, so maybe my smiling family could do it for me.

As he opened his mouth to let loose, we were interrupted by a loud knock.

We both froze, staring at each other, a silent stand-off in the charged environment.

One breath. Two.

I equalised my voice. "Come in."

Felix slipped his head through the door, his brows popping when he took in Ethan—who was not supposed to be there.

"Ah, I didn't mean to interrupt. I was unaware you were with someone, Alica."

I smiled. "That's okay. I was just informing Mr Harris that he's not my client anymore. That you have a vision for the way you want to move forward with his account. And let me say, Felix, Mr Harris can't wait to see what you have planned."

Felix beamed behind Ethan's back as the man in question seethed before me. Only I could see his face, and based on his expression, he wanted to fucking throttle me.

That's right, motherfucker. Get out of my office.

Felix advanced forward and offered a hand which Ethan had no choice but to reciprocate the handshake.

"I look forward to working with you, Mr Harris. I have a spare half hour if you want to come to my office to discuss your account. Alicia's next appointment has just arrived."

Ethan agreed and shuffled out the door behind my boss. Just before he passed the threshold, my ex-lover glanced over his shoulder with a look I had only caught a couple of times before.

He usually locked that openness up tight, loathe to give up any type of vulnerability. But sometimes, his deep-set emotions would filter through.

They were small moments, little snapshots of connection. Sometimes, after we were intimate or when I spontaneously made him laugh.

It was the look of pure longing.

Chapter 10

ETHAN

My hand flexed on the door handle, my body rejecting the thought of leaving Alicia behind.

Instinct warred inside me. I knew the closing of that last physical barrier symbolically came with the close of our relationship.

Alicia had already cut off all forms of communication, and now she had passed me over as a client. I was a complete idiot to think I could waltz into her office and reason with her when I only had unsound reasoning to begin with.

Our previous conversations had not gone how I envisioned, always ending in catastrophe. My intention, coming into her place of work, was not to aggravate the situation further but to reconcile.

Instead, I was rammed straight in the face with a fist full of logic and brass knuckles of reason. The resounding impact made me reflect on everything I'd done.

Overhearing the news about her dad had initially made me pause. I could only imagine the turmoil she was going through. Envisioning my own father in the same position had grief sweeping through me so fast I was nearly winded.

Then, I met her sister, who rightfully called me out on my behaviour. Although they had similar features, there was no way you'd miss the relation based on their character alone—they were both fucking terrifying.

And then there was Alicia. She remained beautiful, but there was a certain exhaustion pulling on her shoulders that I hadn't noticed before.

Absolute shame surfaced as I thought of all the fucked up ways I continued to add to her stress.

I sat before her with complete transparency, pushed back my internal fears and genuinely apologised.

I would do anything to rewind time and change my actions. To shut down the defence mechanism that made me destroy one of the best things to ever happen to me.

Alas, we were in the middle of a warzone, and Alicia was being attacked on all fronts. I wanted to fight for her, but I was a sleeper cell that managed to stab her in the back instead.

The last thing I ever wanted to do was jeopardise her career. I was so short-sighted that I didn't even see the risk of my barging into her workspace and demanding she take me back.

God, I was an arrogant fool.

Taking the loss and absorbing that well-deserved self-disgust, I followed behind a vibrant Felix, who hadn't stopped prattling off numbers and other jargon I didn't pretend to understand.

I was lost in my own shifting thoughts, wondering how I was going to get Alicia to give me another chance when Felix stalled in the entrance foyer.

Jake leaned over the front desk, flirting with the secretary, whose eyes were lapping him up like he was edible. *Yuck.*

Felix called her name in a stern tone, pulling her to the side, no doubt to reprimand his employee. Unfortunately, that left me with Jake, who I had been dodging since our disastrous night out.

He swaggered over and traced a fingertip over his cheekbone. "Damn, what happened, bro?"

I arched a confused brow when he pointed to my face. *Ahh, the bruise that Alicia's plastic cock left behind.* "I got into a fight… and lost."

A strange expression dashed over his face before his cocky smirk returned. "Shit, I would have paid to see that."

I'm sure, asshole.

After that video went viral, I made myself scarce, not wanting to associate with anyone who had anything to do with hurting my girl.

I didn't care how irrational my reasoning was. Jake had baited and riled me up all night, pushing me to say the most outrageous shit.

It was a rude awakening, but I had taken note.

I was the first-string running back for the East Coast Cyclones. *So why did I let the musings of a second-string gunning for my position threaten me so much?*

The alcohol mixed with his arrogance got my back up and I *had* to put him in his place.

Yeah, I can see how ironic that was now.

I had ego issues, commitment phobias and underlying traumas I had to unpack. Because I couldn't bring myself to lose Alicia over my own shortcomings.

Then, Felix cut into our exchange with a fake wide grin. "Go ahead, Jake, Alicia is waiting for you."

"Thanks, Felix, I'm looking forward to working with her. I've heard she's *exceptional.*"

First off. Why the fuck are they all chummy and on a first-name basis? And second, why the ***fuck*** *did that last word have an extra nuance to it?*

I'm gonna kill him.

I didn't say anything, didn't even twitch from my position. If I so much as breathed in Jake's direction, I knew my hands would follow, tightening around his neck.

I didn't know why I had such a visceral reaction, but my senses were blaring on high alert.

Take him out. Take him out.

Jake started for Alicia's office, and before he could turn the corner, he gave me a suggestive wink, licked his lower lip, then disappeared.

The only thing stopping me from charging after him was Felix's hand clasping my shoulder as he continued to babble on as if my world wasn't imploding.

"We're so glad to have Jake on board. He specifically requested Alicia... Said you only had great things to say about her work. We thank you for the referral, Mr Harris..."

A heavy beat pulsed against my temples.

Take him out!

Chapter 11

ETHAN

Answer your phone, baby boy.

I immediately deleted the text and blocked the sender—not that it would deter her at all.

"Is that your mother?" Dad asked.

"How'd you know?"

"I dunno. Maybe it was the cringe when you read the message."

I groaned and chucked the phone on the table. My father had flown over to visit. He said the spontaneous trip was because he missed me, but I knew he had grown concerned.

It had been a month since I had cornered Alicia in her office, and I was a fucking nervous wreck, highly strung and snapping the head off anyone who dared venture nearby. And how could I forget that I was playing *atrociously*.

Alicia still accepted my gifts but refused to engage or even consider talking about *us*.

She remained strictly professional in our interactions, yet her indifference was steadily driving me crazy. I missed so many things about her—that body, her laugh. But what trumped them all was her witty personality.

Alicia didn't know it, but she had unintentionally become my game day lucky charm.

Over the years, no matter her location, she would manage to find coverage to watch me play, bombarding my phone with ridiculous messages. I lived for her commentary. Her humour and nonsensical rants calmed my mind and spirit after a long day on high.

She believed our ritual was a frivolous joke, but to me, it showed her devotion. Alicia didn't particularly enjoy football, but to know she'd sit through a whole game and dissect my sport gave me a certain comfort.

Being so thoroughly severed from her life in one fell swoop took a toll on my mental health and, in turn, my game.

It also didn't help that Jake and his big mouth had started blasting his latest infatuation with Alicia around the team at practice.

"A girl with brains, money and *a tight ass. Fuck, what more could a man ask for?"*

I nearly killed him that day—they said the tackle was unwarranted and completely inappropriate. But what the fuck did they know? They were lucky I didn't chop his fucking dick off for looking at my girl in the first place.

I was progressively losing my mind, and I didn't know what to do. And now, with my mother thrown in the mix, I knew I'd get no reprieve anytime soon.

Which was proven by a new call lighting up my screen with another unknown number.

I growled, pressed reject and turned off my phone.

My parents got married young and had me soon after. With a fresh baby came the reality of caring for one—which was a responsibility my mother couldn't live up to. She soon ditched town, relinquished her parental rights and divorced my father in one swift transaction.

Rudy Harris raised and nurtured me alone.

Which would have been fine if I stayed put and didn't go searching for that elusive maternal figure.

I was thirteen when I found my mother, and she accepted me with a warm hug and false promises.

That was a hard period for my dad and me, but I eventually learnt that the only value I had to my mother was in what I could provide for her.

Audrey Collins, my mother, was a taker. She was *always* number one and only ever contacted me when she wanted something. After years of emotional abuse and manipulation, I finally found the balls to cut her off. If only that dissuaded her petty games.

Alas, my ignoring her always came back to bite me in the ass—usually a lot worse than if I just gave her what she wanted in the first place.

Her *love* was always conditional, and usually came at an exorbitant price tag—financially and emotionally. I tried to distance myself as much as possible, but she *always* found a way.

My mother was the only female who had a role in my life, and she had burnt me so many times I still had third-degree scars that never seemed to heal.

I was tarnished, fucking tainted from my warped view of what I thought women were. All because of the one person who was supposed to love and protect me above all others threw me away like trash instead.

Those toxic memories shifted something in my psyche, solely based on my own personal experience and logic. *If my own mother can treat me so horribly, that must mean* all *women are highly manipulative and self-serving, right?*

"Alicia isn't *her*, son."

My eyes whipped up to my dad, who settled in the seat beside me. We leant back and stared out over my expansive backyard with the ostentatious pool. Despite the extravagant plants and the manicured gardens, it all felt *empty*.

In all my years of growing up, my father never turned bitter or hateful. Audrey Collins had done a number on him as well, but he had overcome those demons in his own way. I wanted to demolish mine too.

I sighed. "I don't know how to get through to Alicia, Dad. She's acting the complete opposite to the woman I know. And every time I open my mouth, I just fuck it up even more."

"You must learn how to communicate, son. You're so used to people kissing your ass. And you're also used to reacting to the fight, the confrontation."

"I don't even know when I'm doing it until I've flipped, and it's too late."

Dad placed a hand on my shoulder, the weight comforting. "When you're hurting, you turn into protective mode. But the problem with that is you end up hurting those around you, which inadvertently means you hurt yourself. You have to get over your superiority and self-entitlement. Get on her level and be *honest*, Ethan. I promise the planet isn't going to explode if you show and tell her how you feel."

I stayed silent, letting his words sink in, knowing he spoke with the utmost love and support. "I know your mum took advantage of you and contributed to the way you process things, but you're an adult now, son. There's only so long you can blame her until you have to take responsibility for yourself... Tell the truth. Be vulnerable. If Alicia's everything you say she is, fight for her, Ethan."

In our last meaningful conversation, Alicia asked me to leave her alone. That request absolutely gutted me.

I wasn't lying when I said I couldn't. I truly didn't think I was able to.

I physically and mentally was incapable of being without her, and the revelation had me paralysed with so many mixed emotions.

The funny thing was, even though I didn't want to admit it—especially to myself—I loved her too.

Maybe not so funny after all.

Chapter 12

ALICIA

I stood on the sideline with Felix, watching the Cyclones complete their practice drills.

My fingers tightened on the folder in my hands as I tried to resist looking at Ethan—again.

He was tenacious, unyielding and... solid.

Nope, don't go there. Do not fucking go there.

Despite my best efforts, I hadn't been able to feed the latent hunger that could only be sated by a certain athlete with a talented mouth and tongue.

I had underestimated the connection of being with someone for four years. Ethan knew my body—what I liked, what I *loved*.

After a couple of disastrous dates, I conceded. They never measured up because they weren't *him*.

I missed my little pink friend, but I missed my real-life big friend more.

And I didn't think I was the only one getting frustrated.

Ethan was playing like shit, and his attitude was even worse. The latest scandal was a video of him going off on a fan for yelling out, "Runaway Girl." Sure, I should have sent that person a personal thank you note, but all the added upheaval of media backlash was fucking with my bag.

Felix was *pissed*, and Ethan didn't seem to care—about his money, his sponsors or losing future prospects. Hence why my boss practically dragged my ass to the stadium to assist his feeble plan of pulling Mr Harris back in line. Felix obviously didn't know him well.

I was hesitant. I didn't want to be in Ethan's orbit again. I didn't want to be in close proximity to the viper who had a particular venom that called to my very DNA.

Ethan continued to regularly send me gifts, and I took them, 'cause why the fuck not? But it wasn't the monetary items that made me pause. It was the accompanying cards attached, always written in his hand.

"I miss your soft hair."

"I miss your jokes."

"I miss my lucky charm."

"I miss licking you clean."

Some of them made me smile, others made me lightheaded, and some made me blush as if I were an untested preteen—not that I'd admit that to anyone, especially him.

"I've got to take this," Felix said before answering his phone and moving further down the field.

His voice ripped me out of my head, which in turn had me processing where my gaze had lingered and stayed. *Damn it!* Intense, soul-altering eyes stared back at me, swimming with so much emotion I had to look away before I was submerged and subsequently drowned.

The team was finished, heading for the changing rooms. They were a raucous bunch as they passed, and I sensed Ethan lingering at the back, creating the perfect scenario for him to ambush me.

However, Jake slowed his pace to walk alongside him, leaning down to whisper in his ear. The exchange would have been normal, except Jake's seedy stare seemed to penetrate my skin.

He hadn't been my client for long, but the fool was starting to irritate me. I wasn't unused to the self-importance those types of men had, but his insecurity and lack of experience were starting to show.

Like all of them, he wanted the world. But Jake had to realise he was a green nobody who was still finding his place—and I was more than happy to put him there.

We were supposed to meet for a business lunch that day, but he cancelled last minute, rescheduling to dinner instead. I was going to tell him to shove the meeting up his ass, except Felix's secretary, Heather, booked him in before I could refuse.

That's when the hissing duo reached me, and Jake spared a smug smile my way.

"We still on for dinner tonight, Alicia?" *Why did that sound suggestive?*

"You got the confirmation text, didn't you?" I snarked.

"Yes, yes. Sorry, I'm just excited. I *can't* wait."

I barely refrained from rolling my eyes at his kiss-ass tone when my attention caught on a frozen Ethan.

My former lover held a firm mask, but I could see the shock sinking in as his gaze bounced between us.

Then, Jake signed his own death note by giving a flirtatious wink.

Everything *exploded*.

Screams, pained grunts and the irrevocable sound of hard fists meeting flesh took over. Time was disjointed as a crowd converged, separating the two blurring figures on the ground.

Ethan stood up. Jake didn't.

Chapter 13

ETHAN

I knew Jake was playing me, yet that logic didn't do anything to curb my temper when he whispered his taunts.

"Geez, she's so hot, isn't she?" he said, his leery stare soaking into Alicia. "I want her, but she's a hard nut to crack. A woman like her—fuck, I'd never fumble that."

I should have been drained and tired from training, but my body was highly strung, ready to jump in for round two.

"She's not yours. She will never be yours," I said.

We were getting closer to Alicia, and all I wanted was to disengage with the dickhead and have a couple of private minutes with my girl. But that was shattered when Jake opened his mouth, spitting the most damning words.

"I'm taking her on a date tonight. How much do you think I have to spend before she puts out? Hell, I don't even care. I bet she's *wild* in bed. I can't wait to fuck that attitude right out of her."

I was balancing on the precipice, close to snapping into a psychotic rage. I knew I had to scale back and take a breather before I *destroyed* him.

I thought Jake would have caught the hint from my tense shoulders to my twitching fingers. But he didn't know how close he was to death.

However, Jake proved he had nil self-preservation by confirming dinner with Alicia. What little resolve I had completely evaporated when he winked, causing a cascade effect.

Red filtered into my vision as my muscles moved on autopilot. I tackled him to the ground and managed to land a few jabs to his ribs, but I barely had two seconds before we were ripped apart.

I pulled against solid arms as Jake remained on the ground, blood dripping from his nose, howling like a little bitch. I didn't even hit his face, the moron.

People ran rampant as I heard our names being called from all sides.

But that's not what held my attention. That's not the reason I wanted to jump back in and hit Jake square in the fucking jaw to add a black bruise alongside that pretty red.

Alicia kneeled beside him, grabbing his chin, turning his head from left to right, assessing the damage.

I couldn't watch, refusing to witness her *care* for him.

"*Fuck this,*" I said before I pushed through the crowd.

Before I could flee, I heard Coach's enraged roar, "HARRIS, MY OFFICE. NOW!"

Yeah, yeah.

I drowned my chaotic thoughts beneath the showerhead, the water cleansing the tense muscles that were stretched to the point of snapping.

Everyone had left the stadium, leaving me to wallow in my own misery. Not that I blamed them.

Coach suspended me for two weeks in response to causing conflict amongst the team. Now, Jake, that mediocre running back was going to get a chance on *my* field. And what made that sting even worse? I was the one who fucking put him there.

I cut the shower, wrapped a towel around my waist and turned for the change room when I caught her silhouette in the bathroom doorway.

Alicia stood ramrod straight, arms crossed tight as she tapped her heeled foot against the tiles.

My dick twitched just at the sight of her. Maybe that wasn't the time to announce she was fucking sexy when she was mad. *Oh, I miss her.*

"What is wrong with you?!"

"There's a whole list, love." *Gonna have to be more specific.*

"Why are you starting shit with your teammates? You're already playing like shit, and now this?"

Alicia started pacing, her heated rants mixing with the condensation of the bathroom. She was so caught up in her ramblings that she didn't notice me stalking forward.

"You need to get help or something, Ethan. Get your head checked before you lose everything."

"I already have."

She yelped at my sudden proximity, and that's when I made my power move and dropped the towel.

Alicia's eyes gaped wide as she catalogued every single inch of my body, hooking on my rock-hard dick. I also didn't miss the way her tongue peeked out to wet her bottom lip.

I groaned. *She is going to kill me.*

"Wh—what are you doing?" she stammered.

"Taking advantage of my assets."

I stepped closer, but she held up a hand and closed her eyes. I stopped dead, not wanting to override her request, even though I knew I could.

"I'm sorry," she said. "I didn't mean to objectify you."

I leant forward until my lips were an inch away from hers. "That's disappointing since that's all I want. Objectify me, love. *Use me.* I was made for you."

Her presence was driving me crazy. She was so close, *so near*, I couldn't think straight.

"I—I can't do this," she whispered, her words rushed and laced with pain.

My heart fell right out of my ass as she abruptly turned her back on me. But before she could race out the door, I caught her hand. I didn't mean to touch her, but I didn't want Alicia to leave like that, upset at my advances.

She was trembling, her fingers shaking in mine.

My neck lowered in shame, my nose sinking into the back of her hair, inadvertently soaking in her signature fragrance that I fucking dreamt about.

"I fucked up bad with you, huh?" I murmured into the loose strands. "But trust me, I'm paying for it now. Since I lost you, I've had to work through some heavy self-reflection, and let's just say I don't like the person I've become. I took you for granted, Ali, but *I can't live without you*."

My lips decided to skim down her neck. I wanted my words to seal into her flesh, to sink into the very marrow of her bones.

"Destroying us has been the single worst mistake I have ever made. Fuck football. Fuck the sponsors. Fuck the deals. None of it matters if I don't have you."

Alicia gasped as goosebumps peppered her skin. But she remained still and silent.

"I know all these realisations are coming too late, but I'm not opposed to begging... Don't go to dinner with him, Ali. Stay with me, *please*."

Alicia cleared her throat. "It's not how it sounds. It's a business meeting, not *dinner*."

"I'm serious, love. I don't trust him with you. This isn't the asshole pro league player talking. This is me, the *real* Ethan."

"I don't know anymore. Before, I would have taken your word seriously. But you cut me down and out so fast. I'm still recovering. Who even *is* the real you?"

"*This* is the real me. I lost my way, but I'm willing to do anything to get back to us."

"Us? There is no *us*. When are you going to accept that?"

"Never. I'll never accept that."

Fortifying her resolve, Alicia inhaled a deep breath, then walked out, leaving me naked, exposed and alone.

Chapter 14
ETHAN

Could I be considered a stalker? Probably.

Would she have a solid case for a restraining order? Definitely. But that's only if I get caught.

Look, it wasn't my proudest moment to follow Alicia to her "business meeting". But I had to make sure she was safe.

There was an innate pressure building inside me, telling me to take note and heed the warnings.

Something sinister was approaching, and I wanted to be prepared to ensure nothing ever touched Alicia again—even if that included me.

When am I going to stop fucking it up with her?

We had always been sexually compatible, and I thought I would use that to my advantage. However, she didn't react the way I expected. She never did these days.

My dad's words relayed back to me.

"Tell the truth. Be vulnerable. If Alicia's everything you say she is, fight for her, Ethan."

And that's what I did. I told her the truth and was the most vulnerable I had ever been in my life. Those statements weren't just meaningless whispers; they were groundbreaking and fucking hard to admit.

"I can't live without you."

I meant them. I had never said those words to anyone nor pledged myself so blatantly. But we were obviously speaking separate languages that the other couldn't understand.

Alicia said I wasn't *listening* when that's all I wanted to do.

Tell me what you want, baby, and I'll give it to you. I'll give you the world.

The waiter ushered me forward, inconspicuously leading me to the vacant table beside Alicia and Jake, a thick partition obscuring them from knowing of my presence.

I slipped the waiter a thick wad of cash for the assist, and he gave a subtle nod and left.

The restaurant was high-end and built for confidentiality. Wide booths with secluding decorative panels created the perfect atmosphere for private business.

Unfortunately for them, I was a frequent attendant due to my own business meetings with Alicia in the past, so I knew which compartments didn't hold sound as well.

Hence Jake's nauseating voice that carried over. "Do you want a glass of champagne, darling?"

"What do I look like to you?" Alicia snapped.

"Well, I'm glad you—"

"It was a rhetorical question, fool. If your answer is anything other than your *financial advisor*, the answer is wrong."

Strained silence followed, and I fought with my gut to keep down the chuckle bubbling beneath.

Jake didn't seem to have the same sentiment. "But. You checked on me straight after Ethan attacked me. I thought—I thought you cared."

"Yeah, about that. Why did you get into an altercation in the first place? I don't think you understand you're a commodity now, Jake. Your face is well-built and pretty enough to get endorsements. I *do* care. I was worried..."

Hmm. I didn't like the sound of that.

"...because you have a photoshoot in two days. I wanted to make sure you didn't fuck up your face and lose your first major deal because you're an idiot."

Oh my god. I was fighting with myself not to break out in full-bellied laughter.

I kind of felt sorry for the guy. Alicia cut him down so quickly he stammered like a schoolboy. I knew that place all too well—except I kind of liked it.

"No alcohol, no pet names. Nothing except business. Capiche?" Alicia said.

I held back a snigger when my phone started ringing. *Shit!*

I rejected the call. *I really must get a new number... but then how will Alicia get in touch with me if she needs to?*

My mother had been blowing up my phone for the past couple of months, her demands progressively getting more aggressive.

No matter how many times I blocked her, she managed to contact me somehow.

My dad told me to charge her with harassment, but I couldn't push myself to do it. Some sick sense of loyalty still lingering for the woman who never gave a damn about me.

Another dial rang through, which I hastily denied. And that's when I saw the countless notifications from random numbers and accounts online—all with the same premise.

Stop brooding and answer your phone.

It's urgent. Don't ignore me.

Why aren't you calling me back?

Baby boy, you're going to regret it if you don't answer me!

A strong sense of foreboding took over as I read message after message. They were a mirrored version of what I had sent Alicia after we separated.

Wow. I had now turned into my mother, and the stark realisation had me gasping for air.

The entitlement. The sheer audacity. I had turned into the monster I had been running from for years.

Shame was all I felt as I made the snap decision to leave the restaurant.

I slinked away like a stealthy ninja, but as I was leaving, I paused at a surge of laughter that came from the entrance foyer.

It was the type of obnoxious laughter from someone who wanted to be heard, *seen*.

And in the middle of an adoring crowd was the she-devil influencer who recorded and blasted my undoing online. Katy—the same one who voiced her strong opinion to the masses and created the Runaway Girl hashtag.

Sure, everything she had said was true. But she also pushed that narrative *hard* and profited handsomely from the deals and partnerships she received from that video.

I wasn't about to accept anyone monetising off Alicia's pain and hurt. Fucking no one.

I remained in the corner, contemplating my next move. *How beneficial would it be if I called that snake out in front of her band of followers? Yeah, it would probably be a disaster.*

But before I could decide further, another notification hit my phone, the message bringing forth a distinct sense of impending doom.

You left me no choice, baby boy.

Chapter 15

ALICIA

"What the fuck, Alicia?! Who the hell were you dating for four years?"

My head was shaking on autopilot. "It's not true..."

I was on a video call with Alexis, her screech ringing in my ears. She had called me as soon as the interview aired.

In the middle of my TV screen was a beautiful, teary Audrey Collins. A mother who had signed away all respect and fucking dignity in exchange for a measly bag of money.

And what did the network want in return? Just the absolute evisceration of her son broadcast on national television—which she was delivering on-brand.

Revulsion crept over my skin as I continued to watch the mindless drivel as strategic tears ran down her cheeks. *Oh, she's good.*

"My son deserted me..." Sniffle. *"I loved and raised him with everything I had, then, he left me destitute. Ethan Harris will always be my baby boy, but he has grown into a cruel man..."*

"I don't know, Ali," Alexis said. "She seems pretty genuine."

"What she is is fucking delusional."

"But doesn't this fit into his whole narrative? How do you know she isn't telling the truth?"

I gave a defeated sigh. "Because I've met her."

My phone had been ringing off the hook, and I had officially missed lunch.

If Felix didn't start fielding my calls, the whole damn office was about to be introduced to an Alicia they had never met before—a hormonal, hangry woman who required chocolate, stat!

With a few minutes to spare before my next meeting, I raided the vending machine, downed some water and raced to the conference room.

I set everything up in rapid-fire sequence, laying out paperwork and linking my phone to the video conferencing system. As I was about to turn on the projector, Heather barged through the door, eyes bulging.

"We have a situation, Alicia."

I rubbed my temples. "Will today never fucking end? What is it now?"

"Ethan Harris' mother is here, and she's demanding to see you."

"Why?"

"I don't know. She said she won't talk to anyone except his personal financial advisor, and she's not leaving until she gets what she wants."

"I've got an important meeting that I'm now late for. Tell Felix to kick her ass out."

Heather flushed. "Well, ahh, he wants you to see her. Before she escalates and makes a scene."

Great. *Ethan Harris had been my client for all of two months, and he was already driving me nuts. First, I had to work with that bigheaded, obnoxious, sexy extraordinaire. Now, I had to deal with his mother?* ***I do not get paid enough for this shit.***

I continued to mutter curses under my breath as Heather looked on with panic. "Well," I snapped. "Go and get her."

Tone down the bitchiness, Alicia, before you lose your job.

I rolled back my shoulders, trying to distract myself from the menstrual pains cramping my abdomen. ***Today is the day from hell.***

A beautiful middle-aged woman stepped into the room, and there was no denying her resemblance to my client. Those piercing blue eyes drilled into me with the same intensity, but hers seemed to have a sketchy gleam to them.

She offered her hand, which I accepted.

"Audrey Collins," she said as introduction. "Thanks for meeting me on such short notice."

"Alicia," I replied. I didn't say it was fine because her toddler behaviour fucking wasn't. "What can I do for you today? You requested to see me?"

We both sat on opposite sides of the table, her fake smile reeking of deceit—which was proven by her next statement.

"I'm here to discuss Ethan's account."

I plastered on a serene expression. "And what exactly do you want to discuss?"

"Everything."

This is a test, right? There is no way this is real. *"Unfortunately, I cannot discuss any client details with you."*

"This is your field of expertise, is it not? So do your job."

This bitch did not just—

Bypassing the bullshit altogether, I discreetly swiped open my phone, which was on my lap beneath the table. Then I called the man himself.

If he wanted mummy dearest to come and fight some arbitrary battle for him, he could be in the firing line because I would not bow down to ***anyone.***

Unfortunately, I had forgotten that my phone was linked to the camera system. But since I hadn't turned on the projector, the receiving end could hear and see everything in the room, yet we couldn't see or hear them in return.

So, in other words, Ethan was getting a prime-time reality episode for free. And I was about to put on the best performance of my life.

If I was in my right mind—or maybe if I'd ingested more sugar—I probably would have realised how unethical I was being. But after the day I'd had, I just couldn't bring myself to give a single fuck.

"I don't know what to say, Audrey—"

"Miss Collins."

Are my teeth cracking? *I thought I could hear them grinding together. "Like I said,* ***Miss****. I cannot give you information on your son's account. Now, if you want to book a meeting and return* ***with*** *him, I would be happy to oblige."*

"Can you at least tell me the percentage I'm entitled to?"

I was almost speechless—almost. "You will have to discuss that with your son."

That seemed to piss her off, based on the way her eyes snapped with an underlying harshness. Then, her mouth turned into a grotesque sneer to match.

*"**Exactly**. He is my son, and as his mother, I am entitled to something."*

What came next, I was not proud of—a knee-jerk reaction to her unhinged demands.

*"Unless he deems it so, you're entitled to **nothing.**"*

"Now, look here, you little—"

I stood abruptly, my phone skidding to the floor. "It's time for you to leave. I have a client waiting. And let me make myself clear. I will ensure you don't receive a single dime without the explicit knowledge and consent from Mr Harris himself." Then, I bent closer and whispered, "Because something is telling me you don't have either."

*I left her flabbergasted, her mouth gaping as I made for the exit and opened the door, ensuring there was no misinterpretation. **This meeting is over, lady.***

Audrey huffed and stomped through the doorway before she paused just outside. From her features alone, I knew she was about to let loose, but it wasn't in my nature to let her.

*"Well," I said. "It was really... **something** meeting you, Miss Audacity."*

"It's Audrey."

"You sure? I could have sworn..." Before I could finish, I closed the door in her red, blotchy face. She was seething.

*I turned and slumped back against the closed door. **Is it time to go home yet?***

That's when my gaze caught on my phone screen, shining up from the ground—the timer ticking on as Ethan remained on the line.

Fuck. *All of this is* ***his*** *fault.*

And since I had already fucked up in monumental proportions, I decided to go for broke.

My spine straightened as I stared directly into the tiny lens—until, I swear, I could feel his eyes on my skin—then I raised my middle finger high.

Who knew my aggressive hormonal reactions would spark the beginning of our story? Not me.

"Is it bad that I kind of feel sorry for him?" Alexis asked.

"I—I don't know?"

"Does he have anyone to turn to while this psycho tells the world how much of a bad person he is?"

I rubbed a hand over my face. "His dad. But I don't think he would want to involve anyone else. Ethan was always closed off about his mother. And you can see why… She's batshit crazy."

Alexis' features fell in concern. "I can see the wheels turning in your head. What are you going to do?"

"I don't… Ah, what should I do? Do I have to do anything?"

Alexis paused, a contemplative look taking over. "You don't owe him anything, Ali. But… if you wanted to reach out to him, that doesn't mean you're giving in."

"Yes, it does."

She didn't know him like I did. If I gave Ethan an in, even a sliver of a chance, he would take that as my admission and bulldoze me to the ground. He was not subtle *or* someone who took things lightly. He was emotive, passionate and fully jumped without thinking of the consequences.

But, despite my best efforts, I still cared for him—*hurt* for him.

Who wouldn't? His own mother was completely unbothered in how her actions were going to *decimate* him.

And they would.

Am I willing to sacrifice my own well-being for his when he has been so frivolous with mine in the past?

Chapter 16

ETHAN

I was a ghost, haunting the halls of my extravagant mansion as the vultures circled the front gates. I found myself in a special type of purgatory that was once considered my home.

There was no escape. I was unable to step foot outside, let alone *breathe* without someone shoving a camera down my throat. The paparazzi were ruthless, calling out slurs, baiting for a reaction. All famished and salivating for the rotting remains of my reputation.

My mother—scratch that, *Miss Collins* had fucked me over *again*. *What have I done to this woman for her to hate me so much?* All I ever wanted was to be her son—to be accepted and acknowledged—without her asking for anything in return.

Now, she had cast the final blow, and any remaining hope I had completely shattered alongside my childlike dreams, confirming everything I already knew to be true.

I'm not worth loving.

I stared down at my plate of untouched chicken when my door opened, then slammed shut.

Oh, hell no! Someone's about to die.

As I bolted upright, my dad came barrelling around the corner, and when his eyes met mine, something in my psyche suddenly snapped. My knees buckled, and he caught me before I could hit the ground, his arms squeezing tight preventing me from completely falling apart.

We sat side by side on the couch, the silence more tolerable than it had been in days.

"I couldn't get a hold of you, son. I was worried."

"I need a new phone. I smashed it when the notifications wouldn't stop coming in."

Dad nodded, his features carved into a look of concern.

He had always been my rock, the one I could rely on and turn to for support. "I'm sorry I brought her back into our lives, Dad. I'm sorry I let her remain a member in mine. I'm sorry I was so *weak* that I gave this person enough power to destroy me."

Dad hung an arm over my shoulders, his presence familiar and warm. "Listen to me carefully, Ethan. You are not weak. And she does not hold that type of power! Audrey has always been a narcissist. That has nothing to do with you and everything to do with *her*. I want you to fight this. Fight for yourself, son. Don't give her any more of you."

Resolve began to take root. She had taken too much, pushed me too far. It was time she paid for the consequences of her actions.

"Where do I begin? I don't even know where to start," I murmured as if I had reverted to a hopeless kid asking his dad to fix everything.

And like any caring parent, Rudy Harris remained solid and resolute.

"Give me your phone, son. Let's make a few calls."

A month had passed.

At times, I was so hopelessly lost I was drowning under the weight of all my fucked up choices. However, there were snapshots of clarity—small reprieves that felt like I was chipping away at the emotional baggage of my past.

Dad moved in. I started therapy. And after some inner turmoil, I finally shoved against those unfounded fears and pressed charges against Audrey Collins.

Her prime time special went viral, causing the demons of media hell to crash down on me. Deals were cancelled, sponsors deserted and I was forced to take leave—"for my own well-being", Coach said.

I didn't blame him. I was mentally wrung out, and that had taken a toll on my game. I was in the middle of a brutal legal battle, the case public and downright messy.

Audrey was conceited enough to think I wouldn't retaliate. But when I finally broke through that invisible hold, the illusion of a mother figure evaporated to display the grotesque monster underneath.

She tried to destroy me. So that's what I intended to do in return.

But despite that absolute shit storm, it was not my greatest source of contention. That was reserved for another—a female who continued to hold my attention and devotion above all else.

Alicia Thorne.

I sat beside the pool, staring down at the substitute phone with trepidation. No one had my new number, and all social media was shut down.

I knew her contact by heart, and I had typed out so many messages I'd lost count.

Temptation became a slow, aching torture.

I was desperate to hear Alicia's voice, to feel her skin. I'd even settle for her scathing words. If I could only steal some small piece of her, to hold and cultivate, it would be enough.

However, every time I went to press send, that dreaded guilt would push forth, preventing the follow-through.

I couldn't bring myself to be selfish. That's all I'd been in the past.

Alicia didn't deserve to be pulled into the chaotic mess of my life. She didn't need a broken, fucked up man-child like me running her down and forcing her into my toxic space.

That's when I vowed I would do more. I'd focus on my healing, develop into a better version of myself. Become worthy of her.

Alicia deserved the world. And that's all I wanted to give—on a silver platter with me on my knees, in my rightful place before my queen.

Hold on for me, love. Just hold on.

Chapter 17

ETHAN

I was on a post-game high.

It was my first time back on the field, and I killed it. Sure, my personal life was still a comedic joke, but when I donned my football jersey and held that ball, a sense of normalcy clicked back into place.

So tell me why that balloon of elation suddenly burst when Alicia walked into *my* fucking changing room with her latest boy toy.

Background noise simmered to a quiet lull, and my raucous team members seemed to melt into the background as all my focus was trained on *them*.

He was lean, muscular and tall, with a pretty face to match... I wanted to punch him. My gaze didn't stray, cataloguing their position, the familiarity of their interaction.

I hadn't seen her for weeks, and I had fantasised about the moment we'd be reunited. What I hadn't envisioned was Alicia's arm casually strung in the loop of some random's elbow. And that's when the unsettling revelation hit—she was *comfortable* with him.

My feet were moving without command, leading me forward until I blocked their path.

"Ethan Harris," I said before I crushed his fingers in mine under the guise of a handshake—both a warning and a declaration.

Stay away from my girl, asshole.

"We're busy. Move," Alicia said, her unimpressed expression drilling into me.

I underestimated her power yet again, my withdrawals returning in full force as I struggled to hold myself back. She was so close that my muscles were spasming from the strain, fiending for her attention.

Then, before I could string a logical thought together, they had pivoted past me to a sidelining room.

His name was Owen, and he was a physiotherapist.

Well, let's see how good he is.

I was the last player remaining, strategically waiting until we were alone so I could question him freely.

"So... How do you know Alicia?" I asked while I was face down on the massage table as he worked on my legs.

"Ah, we went to high school together."

"High school? You must be close..."

"We used to be."

"Used to be?"

That's when he paused, alerting me to sit upright and consider him front-on. His next words had me shocked.

"Her sister is the love of my life, and I'm trying to win her back. Something tells me we're in the same boat?"

Damn, he clocked me good. I had been so consumed in my jealousy that I didn't notice he was suffering from the same affliction as me.

We were both in love with a Thorne sister, and we had both stuffed up.

I shuddered. "I met Alexis once. Let's just say those Thorne girls are fucking scary."

He chuckled. "Scary, but entirely worth it."

"*Entirely.*" I sighed before pulling on my hair. "I don't know what to do. How to fix what I've done."

"Let's make a deal."

Not again. First Burt and now him. "I'm not giving you $50,000."

"Okayyyy, that's specific. But I don't want money. A phone call will do."

"Who am I calling?"

"My brother."

Hmm, that sounds easy enough.

I regret the deal.

Owen had written a full script for me to follow. I didn't even get to read it before the dial tone was ringing with the speaker on.

A teasing male voice answered—his brother, Liam. "What? Shouldn't you be busy licking Lex's asshole or something?"

Owen turned bright red, and I couldn't help but snicker. "Ah, no thanks," I said.

"Who's this?"

"Ethan Harris."

He gave a hasty laugh. "You've got to get better AI, bro." Then he hung up.

Owen watched on with mortification, clearly lost for words.

He needn't be embarrassed; it was the most entertainment I'd had in a while. I shook my head in amusement, deciding to call back via video instead.

Liam answered immediately. "What do you want, shitface?"

I stared into the camera with my most charming grin—the professional, white-toothed smile manufactured for the masses.

He stuttered. "Bro... what type of voodoo bullshit is this?"

That's when I shifted so he could see his brother hovering over my shoulder. Owen had recovered, his features morphing into a smug smirk. Then I said, "Nice to meet you, Liam. I've heard you're my biggest fan?"

A stagnant beat passed, followed by a high-pitched squeal. "Oh my—it's you, really *you.* ETHAN HARRIS! The man himself. Shit, shit, shit." Liam fumbled with the phone before correcting. "Can I take a screenshot of us together?" he asked, his speech rushed and panting.

"I'll do more than that. I'll personally sign some merch for you and your son, but under one condition."

"Anything, man."

I skimmed the paper in my hand, then gave Owen a sarcastic brow. *Really, dude?*

He just gave a resolute nod in return. *Maybe I should have just given him the money.*

I sighed, staring back at the screen, relaying the written message with a robotic voice. *"Next time you open your big bitch mouth, make sure your mini-me parrot doesn't overhear your bullshit."*

Liam froze. For a second, I thought the phone malfunctioned. Until his voice carried through, unimpressed. "*Nice, Owen.* Embarrass me in front of royalty, why don't you."

"You did that yourself, you crude Neanderthal!" Owen yelled, laughter coating his words.

I chuckled. "Anyway, we've got to go Liam, but I'll make sure you get that stuff, alright? Thanks for your support! Great meeting you."

Liam continued to fangirl for a bit, then hung up with the biggest grin. Mine dropped immediately, my cheeks aching from holding the exuberant expression. I loved my fans, but having to be *on* at all times required a lot of energy.

"Doesn't it get tiring?" Owen asked.

My eyes swept up to his assessing ones, his gaze probing my features, all too aware.

"Umm, what?"

"The mask you have to slip on. Don't you get tired?"

And for once, I went with full honesty, with a stranger I had never met.

"You have no idea."

Chapter 18

ETHAN

Owen blew a long, low whistle after I gave a brief rundown on the many ways I fumbled Alicia.

I didn't have to go into detail—as soon as I mentioned the video, he caught on quickly.

"That was about *her*? Bro, you made that shit worldwide," he said, clucking with disapproval.

"You don't think I know that? How do I get her back?"

"You have a time machine?" he asked, his tone snarky and sarcastic.

I stared at him, deadpan. "Huh, funny." *Idiot.*

"Alright. Where are you both at right now?"

I ran a hand through my hair, pulling on the roots. "I don't know. Every time I think I'm making some type of progress, I get iced out. You saw how she was tonight."

Owen crossed his arms, his expression thoughtful. "Well, what have you done to earn her forgiveness? To *show* you are sorry?"

I tallied each act off with a finger. "I've apologised. I send her extravagant gifts I know she loves. I was even vulnerable with her, which I've never been with *anyone.*" Owen's lips twitched as he tried to hold back an amused smirk—which pissed me off. "What, asshole?"

"That's not good enough. How has that addressed your *behaviour*? How do those actions prove that you've changed? That you would never betray her like that again?"

"Because I won't." *Okay, even I can admit how pathetic that sounds.*

He shook his head. "You haven't given her a reason behind your actions. You've shown some regret, flashed some cash and said a few pretty words, but they have no meaning behind them. Get on her level and communicate."

"I've tried," I whined. *Geez, get a hold of yourself.*

Owen held up a palm, silencing me. "She needs more from you. Alicia needs to know *why* you did what you did and *why* you've acted the way you have. Otherwise, what's stopping this from repeating in the future? When you get overwhelmed or when something becomes too much for you, what are you going to do to keep yourself from panicking and lashing out again?"

A sudden clarity shifted as his words sank deep. *Alicia requires reassurance, not empty apologies with half-ass excuses.*

I was initially sceptical, talking with Owen, but his point of view was helpful. I took his advice seriously as he was the only one who knew Alicia on a personal level.

"That makes sense," I said. "Besides Dad and Alicia, no one's ever given it to me straight like that. Thanks for being honest."

"I guess no one else has called you out on your bullshit before?"

I chuckled. "With my face, fame and money? Not quite."

Owen tilted his head, then his eyes softened, almost in sympathy. "I get it. You're used to people kissing your ass, but you're out of touch with reality, bro. The Thornes… they're *real*. None of that fake shit. They're fair and fiercely loyal. And if you stick by them, they will protect you, love you, *cherish you*."

Owen's words took on a whimsical tone as his features morphed in melancholy—the exact reflection of myself ever since I lost Alicia.

"How do I prove all of that to her, Owen? I-I don't know how to do that."

"You have everything you need here," he said, pointing to the middle of my chest. *Cheesy fucker.* "You were with Alicia for four years, Ethan. You *know* her. Dig deep, pull your head out of your ass and think about *her*. Not for what she can do for you or how she makes you feel. But only about *her* needs. *What does she need from you?*"

I was buzzing with all the ideas that were flying through my head, a renewed gusto taking over as I finished my two-minute shower and collected my belongings.

Our conversation went longer than I intended. Most of the stadium had already cleared out except for the clean-up crew.

How can I prove myself to her? How do I get Alicia to trust me with her heart? To believe I will never betray her again?

I twirled a football between my hands, then stalled in the back entrance and watched as Alicia led Owen to a waiting cab. He gave her a light peck on the cheek—which would have previously given me an aneurysm—then slipped into the backseat before the car pulled away.

I was pleasantly surprised by how well Owen and I clicked. I guess I felt akin to him, like we had some underlying connection since we were both trying to win back our girl. He had a genuine nature, and I took his input seriously—which I planned on implementing immediately.

Alicia was on her own, her back to me, standing in the middle of the dark parking lot without a care.

Does she have no self-preservation? I want to spank her so fucking bad. Tease then pleasure her until she submits and learns a damn lesson.

She didn't turn, instead venturing deeper into the shadows. *Oh, hell no.*

On impulse, I raised the football in my hand, cocked back and let that bitch sail through the air. I was aiming to hit the concrete anywhere near her, where she would look back at me with a layer of surprise and slight annoyance.

But of course, my aim was shot to shit, and the ball came down fast on the back of her head. The impact hit hard which had Alicia fall face-first into the ground.

No. No. No. No.

I ran over frantically. *What the fuck have I done? Oh my gosh, please be alive!*

When I reached her, she was already upright, but when I turned her towards me, my breath caught in my throat.

A line of blood dribbled from her brow, where a killer bruise was beginning to form. "Oh my god, Ali, are you okay? I can't believe—shit!"

"Are you the one who chucked that stupid fucking football? What's wrong with you, Ethan? *What the fuck is wrong with you!?*"

"I was just trying to get your attention, not give you a concussion."

Alicia whimpered, which had my hands stroking her face and hair with tenderness. "I'm taking you to the hospital."

"No."

"Ali, love. You must get checked out by medical staff. I'll—"

"I said no."

I huffed, frustrated and scared. I knew that tone all too well. If I pushed, she would pull away.

"Please," I said. "At least let me call your sister. You can't be on your own tonight."

"Do not call Lex. I'm telling you right now, if you interrupt their night and cockblock my sister, I will personally chop your dick off."

"Can't have that."

I gently traced her hairline, wishing I did have that stupid fucking time machine. "God, Ali. *I'm sorry.* Please, let me take you home to my place."

Her eyes narrowed, but I could see a certain haze in them as if she was trying hard to focus.

"I swear, I'm not going to take advantage of you, Alicia. But I'm not letting you drive in this state, nor am I leaving you alone." She paused, thinking over my request, and her stillness made me barrel on. "If you refuse to be seen by a medical professional, please let me take care of you."

Alicia whacked my hand away from her face. "Fine. But you're making me waffles in the morning. With extra cream and that syrup I like."

"*Whatever you want.*" I hovered close as we walked to my car.

Fuck. My first opportunity to make it up to the girl, and I manage to injure her instead. I'm a moron.

I opened the passenger door and made a show of guiding her into the seat. She looked up at me with dubious eyes. "If you try anything on me, Mr Harris, I promise to follow through with that threat."

My hands automatically moved to cover my dick. I knew what she was capable of, and had no doubts about her expertise.

"All above board, Ali. Promise," I said, two fingers subconsciously crossing over before I finished speaking.

Chapter 19

ALICIA

Ethan carried me from the garage into his room, his touch cautious and gentle—the complete opposite of the person I knew.

"Put me down. I'm not an invalid," I snapped, trying and failing to wiggle out of his arms.

"Can you just let me be your knight in shining armour for once?"

I snorted. "I'm not a princess. I'm a *queen*. I don't need no damn knight!"

"Fine," Ethan snapped before depositing my feet on the floor. As soon as he let go, the ground whooshed up toward me.

Solid hands caught me before I collapsed—again.

"Some queen you are," Ethan scoffed. "You can't even stand straight."

Sudden vertigo had me swaying as I surrendered my weight onto him and closed my eyes for good measure. "It's your fault I'm in this mess. You're no knight. You're the villain who stole me away. Don't lock me in your castle, oh, vicious one!"

“Don’t tempt me,” Ethan said before he lifted me onto his ensuite counter, then, began rummaging around.

I refused to open my eyes, wanting to remain in the dark where the world wasn’t dizzy or complicated. Everything was discombobulated, like I was in the middle of a thick fog where everything was hard to process or reach.

Then, there was that voice—*his* voice—always ready to pull me back out.

“Shower, Ali. Then you can rest.”

I grumbled, processing the sound of running water bouncing off tiles. “I just want to sleep.”

“I know, love. Do this for me, then you can have whatever you want.”

I raised my arms, and he read the cue, slowly undressing me.

“Don’t leave me,” I said, unsure if I’d be able to remain upright on my own.

“I’ll never leave you,” he murmured, his tone light, almost reverent.

Ethan led me beneath the water, which cascaded down my back. I felt his soapy hands washing over my skin, massaging into my flesh. That’s when I stole a peek through half a lid.

We were in the shower together, *naked*... and he was hard—*really* hard. But that’s not what made me pause. It was his expression—his concerned gaze trained on my busted brow, never wavering down my body.

“Uh, Ethan... what are you doing?”

“Hush. Let me take care of you,” he said, quiet and soft as if he didn’t want to disturb the small cocoon we had found ourselves in.

A calming presence enveloped us, a subtle understanding that we were at a stalemate, with all our weapons left at the door.

A particular peace soon took hold as I just let everything be. For one night, Ethan could take care of me. For one night, I would let him be the custodian of my well-being.

One night.

Ethan was attentive and caring.

After he dried and dressed me in his oversized shirt, I was deposited in the middle of his gigantic bed while he ran to the kitchen.

We lay on our sides facing each other as he intermittently applied an ice pack to the injured portion of my face.

I could feel my eyes drooping and my speech lagging from tiredness. My thoughts circled one another in a jumbled mess. I felt like I was stuck in some fantasy land where I could live in that blissed illusion with my love—where nothing would ever go wrong.

"I want a doctor to check you out, Alicia."

"No. I just want to stay here... with you. You'll protect me, won't you, *Superstar*?"

Ethan's breath hitched at the familiar nickname. It had begun as an insult—something I called him when his obnoxious nature was out in full force. However, over time, it had soon transitioned into a term of endearment, the title always laced with fondness and a tinge of affection.

But this time, I said it by accident, my tongue loose from my loopy brain. But in using that word, I rendered him speechless. So, I took advantage, cleared my throat and attempted to change tack.

"You know I could sue you for millions of dollars, right?" I teased.

"You don't have to," he murmured. "I'll give it to you now. Just name a price."

There was a certain synergy building between us. Ethan's severe stare penetrated beneath my skin, the stark blue of his eyes shimmering with unspoken pain. He looked as if he was drowning, a continuous hurt beating him down beneath the surface he couldn't breach—where he couldn't breathe.

I don't like it. Take my breath. Take my air. Just don't look at me like that—like you need me to ***live.***

I tentatively raised a hand and smoothed my fingers down his cheek. "You hurt me."

"I know, love. I wish I could take it all back."

"Oh, Ethan. I've been worried sick about you."

"Me? Don't waste your worry on me, Ali. I don't deserve it."

"Even so... I'm sorry about your mum, Superstar."

His eyes widened just a fraction. "You still care... about me?"

"That's stupid. I've *always* cared. *You're* the one who stopped caring about *me.*"

"Ali, you're the only one I do care about. *You're the only one who matters.*"

"You have a funny way of showing it."

"I know, love, but I plan on fixing that. I've been keeping my distance because I don't want you tainted by this crap with Audrey. But once it's all over, I'm coming after you *hard,* so be prepared."

"Harder than you already have? I think you need to learn some new tricks."

"I have some, with the help of a new friend. I've got you, Alicia. Name it, and it's yours."

I sniggered. "Hmm, you do owe me a new dildo. You stole my last one."

"Pretty sure you gave it to me... More like threw it in my face. But I'm more than happy to oblige, love."

Darkness crept in as sleep threatened to pull me under. His hesitant whisper just managed to penetrate through.

"Can I hold you, Ali... Just for a minute?"

"Mm, that sounds nice," I said, syllables slurred and barely making sense.

Yet, he understood. The last thing I processed was being buried in a comforting warmth I hadn't felt in months.

I was safe. I was protected. I was home.

Chapter 20

ALICIA

Throughout the night, whenever I roused, Ethan was there. Two blue orbs burnt with emotion as his stare never wavered from my face, forever lurking and watching like a stoic sentinel.

Stalker creep.

However, as morning approached, he reluctantly fell into a deep sleep.

Ethan's arms anchored around me as his soft snores puffed against my neck. I took one long second to bask in the comforting embrace before I let dreaded reality settle back in.

With the rising of the sun, our impasse had come to an end, and it was time to leave. I slipped out of his hold and sat on the side of the bed, letting my body adjust to the change in position.

I still had a killer headache, and the injured side of my face ached, but as I tentatively stood, my feet were steady.

Riffling through his closet, I swiped some sweatpants and slides, then went searching for my belongings.

My bag was on the couch, and when I checked my phone, Alexis had given me the all-clear to return to the apartment. I was glad she had left for Acacia Falls so she wouldn't have to see my busted face.

That's when a ghastly bang echoed from the kitchen, followed by an impressive list of curse words. I ran in and stopped short before a middle-aged man who I immediately recognised as Ethan's dad. I'd previously noted their resemblance in passing photos, but seeing the man in the flesh—yeah, there was no denying their relation.

Great.

"Who—"

"You must—"

We both blurted at the same time.

I crossed my arms over my chest, self-conscious since I was in his son's clothes, sans bra. I needn't have bothered—he didn't even register my attire. Instead, his gaze hooked on my face, his own blanching of colour when he catalogued my injury.

"Who—who did that to you?" he asked, borderline distraught.

Awkward. I didn't reply. What the hell was I supposed to say?

Either way, I didn't have to answer because he had already come to the right conclusion, his displeasure blatant by the trembling fists at his sides and the potent anger twisting his features.

"*Right*, he's done for."

He shifted, grabbed a frying pan from the cupboard and raced past me in the direction of Ethan's room.

Oh, no.

I followed suit but couldn't keep up. *Damn, old man has wheels.*

When I reached the threshold of Ethan's room, I was already too late.

Thump. "Ahhhh!" *Thump.* "Fuck!" *Thump.* "STOP!"

Ethan's dad was standing on top of the bed, beating the frying pan against his son's ass. It didn't make much of an impact due to the thick blanket protecting Ethan's rear. Although, based on his screams, you'd think he was being murdered.

I had to hand it to Daddy Harris, though—he was giving it his all, which gave me a sick sense of satisfaction, sprinkled with some nostalgic deja vu. I couldn't help it when my mouth lifted into a smirk as I leant against the doorframe, invested in the show.

If only I had some popcorn.

Ethan soon escaped the mattress, chest heaving as he faced off against his father.

"What the fuck, Dad!? Are you insane!? What the hell did I do!?"

Oop. Harris Senior looked like he was on the verge of committing homicide.

"Look at her face! THAT'S WHAT YOU DID!"

Ethan's beady eyes bounced to me, and his whole body pulled taut with awareness. A multitude of emotions played over his features, three taking precedence.

Devastation. Sorrow. But worst of all, guilt.

And his dad had no qualms interpreting *that* little gem. Mr Harris jumped off the bed, ready to destroy his son when I stepped between them.

He huffed. "Don't protect him, girl, he's not worth it."

I shrugged. "Maybe. But it's not what it looks like. I accidentally got hit in the head with a football, then landed on my face."

His brow lifted high in a sarcastic arch. "That's what you're going with?"

"That's the truth."

His attention pitched to Ethan, who looked on the verge of crumbling to his knees. "I'd never hurt her on purpose, Dad. You know this."

"*Again*, you mean," I said with the right amount of sass. "You wouldn't hurt me *again*."

Ethan flinched as his dad offered a charming smile and handshake. "You can call me Rudy."

"I'm Alicia."

"I know who you are—my idiot son's one true love who he let get away."

Well... *shit*.

Rudy drove me home alone.

Ethan wasn't happy, but we gave him no choice. I wanted space, and it seemed like Rudy needed the same.

He kept on whispering a dialogue under his breath. From the few words I did catch, there were a lot of threats and expletives involved. As he pulled up to a set of lights, I caught the tail end of his latest tirade.

"Fucking report him to the police... take him for all he's worth... and he'd bloody deserve it too..."

"Mr Harris?" I interrupted, but the call didn't penetrate.

So I reached out and touched his forearm. "Rudy," I said more assertively. His attention swung to me, his features softening in apology.

I gave a light smile. "Although I'm frustrated at Ethan, it really was an accident. He didn't mean to hurt me."

Rudy rubbed the back of his neck. "I'm scared for him, that's all. He's been working so hard to become a better man, someone *worthy* of you."

I sat silent and dumbstruck, unsure of how to reply—or even if I should.

He read my hesitance and decided to fill the space. "I'm sorry if that's unfair to say, and I know you don't owe him anything. I may be selfish in asking this of you, but I'm going to ask anyway... Please wait for him, Alicia."

My gaze was locked outside the window, but I didn't process a thing. Instead, my ears perked, waiting on his very breath so I didn't miss whatever else he had to say.

"He's hanging on by a thread, and this legal trial is taking a heavy toll. All he ever wanted was to be loved by her, by his own mother. And she didn't even give him that."

Rudy shook his head. "Ethan has dismantled his world as he knows it and is now currently trying to rebuild it up, one brick at a time. It's hard labour, the most torturous kind, but he's willing to do all of that to improve himself."

I sighed. "He's never confided in me. He doesn't tell me anything. He doesn't *trust* me."

"He's ashamed. Ethan has many issues, and I know he lashed out and hurt you because of them. But you're all he wants and thinks about."

I scoffed. *And that's about enough of that.* "He has bigger issues to worry about right now," I said. "Let him focus on the trial. I refuse to make false promises."

Rudy chuckled. "I apologise for my forwardness. I've heard so much about you that I feel like I know you already," he said with a chuffed air as if he was impressed by my scathing reply.

"You are right, though, Alicia. Ethan must preserve his energy. 'Cause if I know anything about Audrey Collins, the worst is yet to come."

Chapter 21

ETHAN

I stood on the outskirts of the conference room, making myself scarce, hiding in the shadows.

There was only one reason I chose to attend the event at Stella Financial Management. And that reason happened to be up on stage, expressing her gratitude into the microphone as she accepted her well-deserved promotion.

Alicia had worked hard to close the deal for Curtis Wright, legendary ex-major league baseball player. And now he'd be wiping his ass with one-hundred-dollar bills for the rest of his life.

The win was monumental, and I was so proud of my girl. She was beautiful, positively gleaming, and I was giddy from the second-hand payoff.

The Thorne family cheered in the crowd, clapping with overzealous admiration, not giving a damn that they were surrounded by some of the richest and most famous athletes on earth. All their attention was reserved for Alicia, their daughter and sister.

Their reactions were bittersweet, and a certain ache registered in my chest at what I had always wished and hoped for myself. But something deeper lingered—more potent and desperate. I should've been there, celebrating next to them.

I wanted to give Alicia a hug, wrap her up tight and kiss her in front of everyone, but I doubt she would want that heat in front of a room full of colleagues and clients.

And that's all my presence would bring.

The day before, the trial against my mother was tied off with one gigantic, showy bow. The public unravelled that shit with speed and finesse—as if my past trauma was curated and made purely for their gluttonous consumption.

Audrey Collins was hit with defamation, emotional distress and harassment. In the end, I was given a restraining order and two million in combined damages.

Let's just say she lost her ever-loving shit. When the verdict was called, Audrey's mask shattered, and the *real* her couldn't be held back any longer—the courtroom was filled with screaming profanities and blatant threats. She even made a beeline for Dad, attempting to throw hands at his "smug face".

To my delight, she was escorted out in handcuffs, the crowd watching on in disbelief. That was the first time in months I had genuinely smiled.

Until now.

I caught my lips stretching wide as my gaze remained caught on Alicia. Unmarked, untainted and *glowing* without my polluted influence.

When I hit her head with that football, I knew I couldn't be selfish and keep her in danger anymore.

Since then, she had tried messaging and calling, but I didn't relent. Then, my dad gave in to my incessant moping, admitting he gave her my number and relaying their short conversation.

I sent one text—the only thing I could at that time. *"Wait for me..."*

I didn't deserve as much, and I had no right. But I asked anyway. My last remaining hope, typed in three selfish words.

I pushed on with my issues and ongoing battles and stayed away. Alicia deserved someone whole. Someone who didn't hurt her, even if it was unintentional.

But this night was one instance where I couldn't resist.

And seeing her face light up as her boss, Felix, and his wife, Stella, shook her hand made the daunting venture entirely worth it.

Alicia wasn't aware I was there, but that didn't matter. I was more than happy to steal a moment for myself.

In a couple of days, she would come to realise the truth of my heart. *Everything there ever was to know about me, she will have access to*—the thought simultaneously daunting and freeing.

I spared one last longing glance and slipped out the door, leaving the celebrations to her.

With my hood pulled low over my head, I entered the café across the road and sat at the lone window seat.

It had become my new spot and hangout, the café staff friendly and discreet. I settled back in the comfortable lounge, prepared to wait hours for Alicia to leave.

I had become her hidden guard and devoted follower. After everything I had been through, I just wanted—*needed*—her to be safe.

Before I could go through the familiar cycle of regret, shame and self-loathing, my senses perked when I watched Alicia sprint from her work building, panicked tears running down her face.

I was on my feet and in front of her within seconds. Then she saw me, my worried expression, and she ran... *for me.*

I caught her and pivoted for my car as she wrapped herself around my frame. She cried into the base of my neck as my hand ran down her hair.

"Shh, Ali, love. I've got you. I've got you," I whispered. "Whatever it is, we will figure it out."

"*We?*" she asked, all hopeful, which was quickly followed by a loud hiccup.

That's when Alicia leaned back and gave me her devastating face. She was so breathtakingly stunning, even when marked with sadness.

Don't cry, baby.

My fingers raised, chasing away the tears and cradling her face—as if I *worshipped* her. Which I fucking did.

I nodded.

"*We,*" I reaffirmed, infusing that one word with all-consuming love and the promise of *us.*

Chapter 22

ALICIA

Hours had passed, and I was growing weary.

I'd sent my family home after I received my accolades and desperately wanted to join them, but I was technically still on the clock—expected to network and schmooze clients who only came for the free food and booze despite most being millionaires themselves.

The celebration was primarily for Stella Johnson, Felix's wife and General Counsel of the company. She had been on maternity leave with their second child over the past two years and was making a comeback. I was happy to see her return.

Stella was the one who advocated for my position and brought me into the fold. She was the original girl boss I aspired to be. She had my utmost respect and loyalty.

However, even with the ongoing celebration and promotion, all I could think about was Ethan. Despite the successful outcome of his trial, I knew he must be hurting.

I didn't know why I held some sick sense of responsibility or concern, but against my better judgement, I couldn't help but care.

That's when my gaze caught on an eager smirk from across the room. Jake leant against the wall, beady eyes dancing over my frame as if imagining me naked. *Nope. No, thank you.*

I had cut ties with him, palming his contract off to a subordinate over his insistence to push against boundaries that I had set and reminded him of on multiple occasions.

Jake thought he was cute; I thought he was disrespectful. And that's the exact word I used when debriefing with Felix.

On that note, I was ready to leave.

I sidelined the main conference, then swept into the elevator, ascending to the top floor.

The place was empty. As I grabbed my belongings from my office, a crash rang out from the photocopy room down the hall, shortly followed by a pained grunt.

I hope no one's hurt.

Of course, I went to investigate, but as I approached closer, an internal alarm blared through my senses.

Turn around. Leave. Save yourself.

That's when I heard their voices. Both recognisable and coated in lust, their words echoing down the corridor in shallow pants.

"This is the *last. Fucking. Time.* You hear me? So make it count."

"Please, Bossman. You know how much I need you. You know I can't live without it."

By then, my feet were moving of their own volition. My heart wanted to shut out everything and remove myself from the soul-destroying situation. However, my nature wouldn't let me leave without witnessing the irrefutable truth.

So when I silently pushed the door open, I shouldn't have been railroaded from the most disturbing sight—yet I was totalled all the same.

There was my boss, Felix, fumbling with his clothes as Heather—*his fucking secretary*—lifted herself on top of the photocopier machine, pulling up her skirt to show her bare beneath—the display wanton and downright *disgusting.*

They were so caught up in each other they didn't even notice I was there. And from the look on their faces and the confidence of their actions, it wasn't the first time.

Utter revulsion swirled in my gut as bile rose to the back of my throat. Only a few seconds had passed, however, I knew the imagery would scar me for life.

Then, Felix unzipped his trousers, which had me jolting out of my inanimate state to yell the first thing that came to mind.

"I quit!"

All I processed was their shocked features before I bolted straight out of there.

Crashing into the elevator, I slammed my finger against the button, exhaling a grateful breath when the doors closed before either of the cheating scumbags could catch up.

I didn't want to give them any opportunity to talk me down and *lie* straight to my face. *I know what I saw.*

As soon as I reached the ground floor, I ran for the foyer doors. My escape was in reach, so close I could feel the outside air drifting through the shifting glass.

But destiny had other plans.

"Alicia! Alicia! Are you okay?"

Arms caught me in a tight squeeze as soft hands ran over my shoulders in comfort—from the very woman I wanted to save.

Stella regarded me with genuine concern, her gaze cataloguing my anxious state.

When I didn't reply, her expression filled with worry. "Let me find Felix. He's upstairs in his office."

I vigorously shook my head. *No. No. No. I don't want to hurt you.*

"I'll only be a minute," she said, tone reassuring. "I'm going to find him."

As she went to pull away, I latched onto her forearm, unrelenting and firm.

"Don't go up there, Stella," I managed to choke. *Oh, god.*

"Why?" She tilted her head, waiting for further explanation as tears gathered in my eyes. I closed them, not wanting to observe her devastation firsthand.

"*Please,*" I begged. "I don't want you to see that. *To see them together...*"

One debilitating heartbeat later, I was pulled into a crushing hug—one full of warmth and understanding.

"It's too late for that, Alicia," she whispered against my cheek, her tone brittle but firm.

That's when I raised my arms to return her embrace.

Am I in some alternate universe? Why am I the one crying, mourning the loss of a marriage in the arms of the wife it belongs to?

Stella slowly withdrew as I sniffled, failing to regain control.

"I told them I quit on the spot," I said. "I know firsthand what that type of destruction can do to someone, including their family and loved ones. These terrible deeds have a cascade effect, and I can't knowingly respect and work under someone who chooses to live their life like that. *I refuse.*"

It was a bold statement, but I meant every word. Living alongside my sister for four years and having a front row seat to her ongoing turmoil ingrained something deep inside me. And seeing Felix blatantly cheating in 4D—while celebrating his wife in the same building—solidified my resolve further.

Stella gave me a sad but knowing smile. "Thank you for being sincere in a world that tramples the weak, Alicia, but I want you to stay in the company."

"I can't work for him."

"He won't be your boss for much longer. Will you stick around to see what happens? I promise your new boss would love to have a loyal employee like yourself."

I shifted over her words, receiving the underlying message. I refused to remain for him, but maybe I could stay *for her*...

"If you do decide to stay here, Alicia, I only have one request. Please keep this *discovery* to yourself... for now."

Discovery—meaning the inappropriate love affair between her husband and his secretary.

I cringed. "How long do you want me to wait? I'm not a good actress."

"You will know when," she said with full authority and power.

That's when I took her in, really perusing the superwoman before me.

Sure, I could see the hurt swimming in the depth of her eyes, but that was overshadowed by her poised persona. She was all class and grace, a savage undertow lurking beneath.

That's when it all clicked. Stella garnered respect. Not Felix or the business. *Her.*

Pitching forward, I tackled her in another hug and whispered. "Welcome back, boss."

She chuckled, which was interrupted by my name being frantically called from behind.

Felix.

I didn't spare him a thought, my eyes refilling with tears as I stared at the indestructible woman before me.

Stella gave my hand a light squeeze. "Go home, Alicia. Spend time with your family."

"I don't want to leave you here with him."

"I have plans... Plans that have not come to fruition yet. I need you to leave," she said, all cryptic.

In other words—*don't fuck this up, Alicia.*

Whatever strategy she had devised, I knew Felix deserved everything that was coming his way. And it was not my right to take away from Stella's experience and hijack her hurt.

So, taking her request seriously, I swept a light peck to her cheek then raced out the door before Felix could reach me... Sending all my strength to the woman with a spine of steel and the assassin's smile.

Chapter 23

ALICIA

I don't know why Ethan was outside my work building, but I didn't question the timing or his presence. He was there when I needed him the most and held me together as I fell to pieces.

We were in the driver's seat of his car, my legs straddling his lap as my face buried in the base of his neck—a rookie fucking move.

Why does he have to smell so good? And why do I feel so safe in his arms?

Ethan rhythmically ran a hand up and down my spine, unfurling my tense muscles, whispering sweet words into my hair.

It felt good, *too good.*

"What happened, Alicia? *Who hurt you?*"

I huffed non committedly, then burrowed deeper into his chest. I shouldn't have, for his rigid shaft pressed against my centre like the worst tease known to mankind.

"No one hurt *me*. I was just... just..."

Ethan shifted back, his roaming fingers lifting my chin until I had no choice but to stare into his desperate, pleading eyes. "Just point me in the right direction, Ali. I'm your weapon. Use me as you will."

Heat surfaced beneath my skin, gathering to the apex between my legs, lust coating my insides, imploring him to enter. *Down, girl.*

I coughed. "You just went through a highly public trial. I think you running in to defend my honour would be untoward."

"I don't care, as long as you're safe and happy," he said, his mask taut with anguish. "I never want to see you cry again."

My head tilted, perusing the man I did not recognise. He was my old Ethan mixed with someone entirely different.

"What's that look?" he asked.

"Hmm, just trying to figure out what you want from me."

"*Everything...*"

My lips pursed, the sincere declaration had me out of sorts. Right then, in the cradle of his embrace, I felt his true intentions and knew them to be real. But I'd been conned by him before, and I experienced firsthand how far that fall could be.

Reading my expression, Ethan delicately traced my hairline, his touch searing.

"I deserve your hesitation. And I understand your unwillingness to believe in me. But that's the truth, Ali."

Then, Ethan initiated his finishing move by giving me his cheeky smirk with the added twinkle in his eye—his expression all the way mischief with a side of sexy.

Someone help me with this magic voodoo shit! I repeat... SOS!

My tongue licked out to wet my bottom lip, wishing I was sucking on his instead. Ethan's expression darkened in reply, his thumb chasing the moist edge as if imagining the same.

"There's my girl. No more tears," he said, voice low and husky.

"I'm not your girl."

"Let a man *dream*, Alicia. Don't cut my heart out so quickly."

"You have a heart?"

"Only one that beats for you."

My brows furrowed at the conflicted feelings racing through my body.

On one side, there was pure elation after hearing what I had coveted for so long. However, all my previous humiliation and pain had left a lasting impression, making me weary to fully accept him.

What am I supposed to say to that?

I disengaged from his lap and dropped into the passenger seat, creating space to breathe. I couldn't think straight when he was so close.

"Can you—can you take me home?"

"Of course, Ali. I'll take you wherever you want to go."

Despite the charged atmosphere, the drive to my apartment building remained silent.

But when Ethan parked and I made to leave, a warm hand grasped mine, quietly begging me to stay.

Please, let me have the strength to leave this car.

Slowly—*ever so slowly*—Ethan leaned over the centre console and pressed a light kiss to my lips. It was chaste, barely existent, but that one point of contact was filled with so much promise and desperate yearning he had me reeling.

"Why did that feel like a goodbye?" I whispered, his tortured face hovering before me as my lips tingled with a roaring need for more.

His baby blues swept over me in urgency as if trying to memorise each feature, every microscopic line.

"I don't know how you'll feel about me after tomorrow night. So I had to be selfish and taste you one last time."

My pulse gave an almighty thump. "Ethan... *what have you done?*"

"Something I should have done a long time ago. Just—if—if you choose to never speak to me again. Will you send one last message? A single text to say goodbye... so I know."

After everything that transpired between us, he had *never* given up. The talk of farewells and alluding to future hurt had my lungs seizing in my chest.

My fingers squeezed around his. "You're scaring me."

"Don't be scared, love. Just promise me... one text, Alicia."

He was serious, purely based on his stubborn mask that seemed to solidify with each passing second. I didn't have the energy to push back against it.

I was overwhelmed and emotionally exhausted. I wanted my apartment, my family and my favourite oversized hoodie—that may or may not have formerly belonged to the man staring back at me like he was *dying*.

Nope, don't go there.

"Okay," I said, conceding. *For now.*

Ethan simply lifted our joined hands and kissed the back of mine before he murmured, "*Goodbye, Alicia.*"

I detached myself and walked into the foyer, spine straight, gaze forward. I knew if I looked back, gave into that one glance, I'd run back to his side and never leave again.

But when I heard his car pull away and disappear in the distance, my soul screamed out, and my body followed suit.

Firm, weathered hands held onto my trembling frame, shepherding me into the elevator.

"Burt? Is love worth all this heartache?"

He pressed the button to my floor and gave up a sympathetic but genuine smile. "Always, kid. I'd do anything to relive those times with Imogen. Even the bad ones. She was worth all the heartache… Is *he*?"

Chapter 24

ETHAN

My gaze flicked from the overhead lights to the encroaching camera lens, nerves simmering through my system, begging me to up and leave immediately.

"Are you comfortable, Ethan? Do you need anything before we start?" Veronica asked, leaning forward in the chair directly across from me.

She looked sincere despite the tense environment. The television crew had created a simple setting for our one-on-one interview. The room was minimal, with two chairs and a side table for water. That was it.

I didn't want a big show and dance. Just a platform where I could tell my story in the most transparent and straightforward way possible.

And as one of media's leading journalists, there was no way Veronica was going to pass up the opportunity to interview Ethan Harris—especially at the height of his legal battle with his own mother.

Frankly, I didn't care who was on the other side asking the questions, as long as they were in direct competition with the network that interviewed Audrey.

An assistant behind the scenes called out a two-minute countdown before we were live.

My hands clenched into fists on top of my thighs, in an effort to stay my trembling limbs.

I knew this was a gamble, addressing everything on such an open forum. But I wouldn't be who I am if I didn't settle this the way it started. The time had come to address my issues just as publicly as I had back then.

To bolster my confidence, my memory relayed valuable pieces of advice that left a lasting impression, from both Dad and Owen.

"There's only so long you can blame your mother until you have to take responsibility for yourself... Tell the truth. Be vulnerable. If Alicia's everything you say she is, fight for her, Ethan."

And that's what I intended to do—fight to the fucking last for my girl.

"She needs more from you. Alicia needs to know why you did what you did, and why you've acted the way you have. Otherwise, what's stopping this from repeating in the future? When you get overwhelmed or when something becomes too much for you, what are you going to do to keep yourself from panicking and lashing out again?"

Ever since I had lost Alicia, I had initiated a change for the better. Sure, I was in the preliminary stages and still had a long way to go, but she was at least owed an explanation and an honest apology.

"Ethan?" Veronica asked, pulling me back to the present. The chamber was silent, everyone waiting for my reply as I'd missed the cue—the cameras were rolling.

Showtime!

Readjusting my posture, I gathered my thoughts and settled my attention on the task before me. "I guess I'm a bit nervous. I don't know where to start."

"How about from the beginning?"

I inhaled a deep breath, then blew out slowly. "I was fourteen years old when I realised my mother didn't love me..."

After relaying my volatile history with my mother, Veronica began her probing.

"Ethan, after hearing about Audrey and the influence she had on your life, a lot of people at home will be wondering... Why didn't you just cut her off?"

"I wish the answer was that simple, but it's so complex. We don't have enough time to break down all the ways my mother fucked with my head," I said, tapping a finger to my temple. "*But...* with recent events, I've been trying. It's hard to explain, but with the help of my therapist, I'm starting to understand a lot more about myself."

Veronica gave a subtle nod, encouraging me to continue.

"When my mother deserted me, then continuously treated me like trash, it changed something in my psyche. I constantly searched for her validation, unintentionally giving her the key to my own self-worth.

You know"—I gave a half-ass chuckle in self-deprecation—"when you feel you've been abandoned by your own mother, this maternal figure who is supposed to love and protect you no matter what, it leaves a gaping hole. I unconsciously tried to fill that, knowing damn well she was never capable of being that person."

"And how did that influence other relationships in your life?" Veronica asked.

"Since childhood, I've held the deep-seated belief that people either leave, take advantage *or* betray me in some way. Thus, I developed dysfunctional behaviours to cope with these innate fears."

Veronica's eyes widened in sympathy. If she wasn't someone who gained a paycheck catering to the masses, I probably would have believed her. "Can you describe these behaviours and how they would manifest?"

I shrugged. "Just the usual harmful bullshit. I actively pushed people away to avoid getting hurt. And I've always had difficulty with trust—to the point that I was hypervigilant and paranoid of others' motives. I would frequently hide my true feelings or withdraw from uncomfortable situations rather than communicate effectively. But if I felt especially vulnerable or exposed, sometimes, that would manifest into anger."

"Would you say that these behaviours played a role in your romantic life as well?"

"Most definitely. I always rejected the idea of an intimate relationship. I didn't want that type of connection—to give someone that much power over me. The mere thought was terrifying."

"And what about now?"

"Now, I'd give anything to have that."

Veronica gave a soft, teasing smile. "Would this drastic change have anything to do with that viral video?"

My spine straightened, giving all my focus to the most important part of the interview. "It has *everything* to do with that. My actions in that video served as the catalyst for me losing it all."

"What do you mean by *all*?"

"It means I lost the most important person in my life, *Runaway Girl*."

Chapter 25

ETHAN

"Can you talk us through that video, Ethan?"

Heat raised beneath my skin, flushing my cheeks. "Shit, that's just one piece of the puzzle... I'm ashamed to say my atrocious behaviour didn't start there. That just happened to be the part that was memorialised on film."

I shifted uncomfortably. "Honestly, I look back on that video with self-disdain. I didn't protect or keep my girl safe. Instead, I was acting like a complete *cunt*—oh, shit! Can I say that?"

Veronica suppressed a laugh. "You can say whatever you want."

I ran a hand through my hair, embarrassment creeping down my spine "There is no excuse for the way I behaved, and I wish I could take it all back.".

"Why did you behave like that? What happened to make you react that way?"

"She said she wanted a future with me," I said, my tone wistful and full of regret. "And because of my avoidant attachment issues,

I panicked—then self-sabotaged the healthiest relationship I've ever had."

Veronica tilted her head in reflection. "Are you sure it was self-sabotage? And not a common case of '*you don't know what you've got until it's gone*'?"

I shook my head. "I can see how people would think that, and I guess there is *some* truth to it. But even *I* can admit our relationship had already taken that next step—before I turned it into a disastrous train wreck, of course. I... I never told her this, but I wanted her to meet my dad. The next time he was due to visit, I was going to introduce them..."

"Is that significant? Meeting your father?"

"For a commitment-phobe like me? Yeah, it is." I smirked, my eyes catching on my dad, who stood in the corner of the room, face gleaming with pride. "For a long time, Rudy Harris has been the only one given full access to my inner sanctum. But unbeknownst to me, in the last four years, another has managed to infiltrate those walls."

"And then the video happened?"

I caved in on myself, my head downcast as I tried to find reprieve from the glaring vulnerability. "And then the video happened..."

Veronica shifted and raised a tablet between us. "Should we watch that video back so we can talk about it?"

I didn't have to. I knew every line, each dreaded frame by memory—as every single second of that two-minute clip was burnt into my fucking brain.

Despite that, I gave a resolute nod, allowing my disgusting behaviour to play out. Utter revulsion swept over me in waves as each scathing word hit me with another swell.

But that was the whole reason why I was there, why I had agreed to the exclusive interview. So I could address and debunk each piece of filth that flew out of my mouth.

I don't deserve Alicia—I never did—but I'm hoping, with the actions I'm taking now, that I'm beginning to.

Once the scene was complete, Veronica tucked the screen away and stared at me expectantly. Like she was the fucking judge and jury of my fate.

Nope. That's reserved for one person only.

"Ethan, how did you—"

I raised a hand to cut her off. *This is my show now.*

"I'm going to flip the narrative on this one. I know that's on the internet *forever*. So we're going to go through each damning statement again. And then I'm going to replace that with the *truth*. We good?" I asked Veronica, borderline rude.

She just swept her hand in reply, giving me the signal to go ahead.

Then I hit replay.

"...The bitch wants me to marry her, she's delusional. In all these years, I haven't even acknowledged her in public..."

"One. She isn't delusional. *I am.* I was an immature fool who feared my past. Now, I'd do anything to have her on my arm, to show her off to the world, to claim her in front of *everyone*."

"...She's a good girl that listens to everything I say... No commitments means no demands and no expectations. I get whatever I want, whenever I want..."

I sniggered at my blatant show of overinflated ego. "Look, there's no way to sugarcoat this, but I completely assassinated her character here—especially since she is *nothing* like I just described. They're lies."

"... When I tell you this girl isn't even marriage material, let alone mother material..."

I slumped back, a reluctant sigh passing my lips. "I still can't believe I said such vicious things about her," I murmured.

"Can you repeat that, Ethan? We didn't quite catch what you said?"

Negative emotions began playing havoc with my thought process as I tried and failed to recompose myself.

Remember your why, Ethan. Think of your why.

That's when Alicia's smile flashed through my mind, her expression open with so much affection shining from her eyes, I knew I'd do anything to have that back.

With reinforced belief, I rolled my shoulders, sat upright, then locked my gaze on the closest camera, imagining Alicia behind the lens, wishing and fucking hoping that she could feel my sincerity.

"*Now I'm speaking directly to you, love.*" I said before I cleared my throat for dramatic effect. "I want you to know that all my fucked up actions leading up to this point has nothing to do with you and everything to do with *me*. It's *me* who isn't husband material. It's *me* who isn't father material." Unsolicited tears began to gather in my lash line. Yet, I didn't seem to care. She deserved to see it all. "Fuck. If only I was so lucky to have you as my wife, as the mother of my children. I once told you that *nothing else matters if I don't have you*. And you can fucking bet your ass that I'd give up *anything* for the honour of you taking my last name and becoming my family."

Veronica gave an approving nod as light cheers infiltrated from the offset, soon followed by one overzealous hoot—which I was betting was my dad.

The cameraman silently counted me down, dropping a finger for each remaining second I had on air. I didn't budge, my gaze drilling into the lens, my final lifeline.

Hear me, love. This is for you. All of this is for you. Everything I do is for you.

"To the world, she's known as Runaway Girl. When all I want is for her to *run back to me*. Don't walk, baby, sprint full-speed, run as fast as you can—because I fucking swear, I'll catch you this time!"

Cut. Time was up.

Chapter 26

ALICIA

"Quiet! Quiet! My show's about to start!" Alexis screamed over my parents, who were bickering in the kitchen.

My family came to the city to celebrate my promotion, then decided to stay the rest of the weekend.

I hadn't realised how much I missed them until my apartment was filled with constant teasing and off-tune singing.

I sat in the corner of the couch, my nephew snuggled in my lap as I buried my nose in his hair. Austin wasn't one to keep still for long, but I was a master negotiator and bargained with chips and chocolate—he was currently stuffing his face.

Alexis side-eyed me, fiddling with the remote. "Did you have to give him junk food so late? He's going to have a sugar high before bed."

I poked out my tongue, which Austin immediately copied. "Leave my boy alone," I said, cuddling him closer.

Alexis huffed when our parents walked in, my mum shaking her head as Dad followed behind like a lost puppy.

Harriot Thorne was currently giving her husband a lecture on clean eating after he was caught sneaking a thick slice of cake. After his stroke, Mum had taken it upon herself to be his main carer and primary supporter. Which also meant she was the boss.

Sure, she was overprotective and manic at times, but Dad was making a remarkable recovery, surrounded by those who loved and cared for him.

Defeated, he collapsed on the couch beside me, grumbling under his breath. Incognito, I pulled a spare candy bar from behind the cushion and slipped it under his arm.

His face lit up before he gave a cheeky wink, sliding the gift into his pants pocket.

That's when Alexis gave a sharp gasp, turning up the volume on the TV. Before I could ask, *his* voice rang through the room as if he were right there with us.

"I was fourteen years old when I realised my mother didn't love me..."

Ever since we had parted ways the night before, I had been ruminating on the meaning behind his goodbye.

I never would have guessed that he was referring to a live national television interview.

My eyes were glued to the screen, cataloguing each expressive feature, trying to distinguish if it was truly real.

Ethan was breathtakingly open and raw as he relayed his traumatic past to the world. I couldn't help but be proud of him.

Despite the public domain, I knew he was doing it for *me*.

Everything seemed to fade into the background as my attention was solely placed on him, soaking in every sentence, absorbing each revelation.

My heart ached for the little boy he described, and for the man who lost his self-worth chasing after a delusion.

Ethan was resolving all my unanswered questions, providing reasons for why he reacted the way he did. But also gave resolutions on how he wanted to change and the actions he was initiating to make that happen.

There were no excuses, just the bare truth, his vulnerability both brave and awe-inspiring.

Then, I swear my useless organ of a heart nearly gave out when he mentioned Runaway Girl.

That dreaded video, his explanations, the hurtful words he replaced with meaningful ones. They had me unravelling.

"Now, I'm speaking directly to you, love."

My breath hitched in my throat.

"Oh my—Holy shit, Ali! What are you going to do? He just said..." Alexis continued to rant as my brain misfired.

Who is this man?

I continued to listen with single-minded rapture, not wanting to miss a moment.

"Ah, Aunty... you're hurting me," Austin said in a low whine.

That's when Mum's concerned voice filtered through. "Are you alright, Alicia? You look like—"

"Like me when I was having a stroke." Dad cut in, crowding into my space. "Are you okay, Ali? You're pale—trembling, even."

I immediately released Austin, who I'd unintentionally squeezed into a tight grip, then jumped up, pressing closer to the screen.

Their voices filtered into a buzzing static as Alexis seethed. "Shut up and let the man speak!"

"To the world, she's known as Runaway Girl. When all I want is for her to run back to me. Don't walk, baby, sprint full-speed, run as fast as you can—because I fucking swear, I'll catch you this time!"

When the end credits began rolling, my knees were already on the floor, my legs refusing to hold my weight.

"Someone tell us what the hell is going on?!" Mum asked. "Who is that man?"

Austin continued chomping on his goodies as he enlightened my parents. "I thought he was my daddy, but Mama said he wasn't father material, just like he said on TV. What does that mean?"

All eyes pivoted to Alexis, including mine.

She raised her hands. "I saw him outside your office in the early days of his betrayal. And he was acting smug as if his fame could get him out of the hole he'd dug himself."

"And what do you think now, Lex?" I asked, voice low and strained, on the verge of being defeated.

Her features softened, genuineness shining through. "I think he's putting in the work, Ali. I think he's doing everything he can to be worthy of you."

Mum stepped closer. "Alicia, who are you to that man?"

"*I'm* Runaway Girl."

Pause. "And... are you going to run back to him? Like he asked?"

"I-I don't know..."

"Do you want to?"

"*Yes.*" The answer was so immediate that the response was out of my mouth before I could compute.

That's when the unsettling realisation fully took root. I had already forgiven him.

It was both gradual and all at once.

Ethan's subtle pleas, his silent support, the guarded protection. After so many months, I had softened towards him.

I missed us together. I missed my friend and lover.

The night before, I had asked Burt if love was worth the heartache. I hadn't been able to get his answer out of my head. Despite all of Ethan's wrongdoings, I, too, was willing to push through the bad times to relive the good ones.

"*Well.*" Dad scoffed, cutting into my thoughts. "He has to go through *me* first. He can't just say a few words on TV and act like everything is fine."

Mum sighed. "You heard what he's been through, Phil."

"And I heard what he said about Ali, too."

I rubbed my temples. "Dad, I'm a grown woman."

"So what? You're still my baby. He has another thing coming if he thinks he—"

"Mum." I interrupted. "Dad's got a chocolate bar hidden in his pocket."

Stark betrayal flashed in his eyes as Mum's narrowed on him.

"Every man for himself." I winked.

Crisis averted. For now.

Chapter 27

ETHAN

As soon as the interview aired, I was back to being the golden boy, my desperate pleas resonating with the equally afflicted lovesick fools and star-crossed lovers.

Runaway Girl had turned into *#runbacktome*, the hashtag trending and taking over the internet. The masses rallied for reconciliation and a happily ever after.

Oh, how I wish for that too.

However, I was yet to hear from Alicia, and the dead space had my nerves peaking. I didn't know whether to be grateful or alarmed that that goodbye text hadn't come through. But every minute that passed without it had a certain hope blooming in my chest.

My fingers drummed against the steering wheel as I pulled up to the stadium, a crowd of paparazzi swarming the gates. It was packed—a lot more than usual.

I slowed to a crawl, not wanting to run over some guy's toes and get sued for the inconvenience.

But as my car rolled past, the reception caught me off guard. Invasive, flashing lights came from all directions, their screams penetrating through my safe, steel bubble.

"What's the important announcement, Mr Harris?!"

"Ethan! Ethan! Does this have anything to do with your most recent interview?"

"What's so important you called a press conference *before* the game? HARRIS! HARRIS!"

What are they talking about? Maybe Coach has set something up?

With a confused scowl, I left their questions behind, parked up, then made my way to the back entrance reserved for staff.

However, with each step closer, my muscles seemed to tense as a charged energy set off my intuition.

Something's wrong. Something's wrong.

As soon as I breached the door, I was jerked sideways, blindly pulled into a darkened alcove.

"Come with me, *now*," rushed a familiar voice. My gaze snapped to Jake, who continued to grip my arm.

I whacked his hand away with bruising force, the impact causing him to hiss in pain.

"Don't fucking touch me," I seethed through clenched teeth.

Yet, he didn't seem to get the memo as, despite my threat, he still blocked my way. "You *will* follow... unless you want me to lay this on your *Runaway Girl* instead?"

It was the way he said it—his tone intentional, provocative and *knowing*. I had to find out what he knew because, based on his expression, he had some type of knowledge. And he was ready to use that to invoke maximum damage.

Not if I have anything to do with it.

"Hurry the fuck up before I beat you to death."

Jake clucked as he turned down the deserted corridor, leading me further into the catacombs of the stadium, where staff would not venture or find us.

My thoughts rattled against one another, thinking of all the scenarios that could play out. Despite the million that came to mind, there was no way I could have prepared for the one presented.

Jake directed me into a makeshift office, and once I was inside, the door slammed shut. On instinct, I turned, finding two identical smirks.

Obnoxious, wicked and fucking ugly.

Jake and my mother, Audrey Collins.

"I've missed you, *son*."

Tension rattled my insides, underlying rage threatening to unleash on the fools before me.

With faux ease, I swaggered to the opposite side of the room, placing a generic wooden desk between us.

"To what do I owe the pleasure?" I asked, all nonchalant, as if my fight-or-flight response wasn't wreaking havoc through my nervous system.

But it was all worth it when Jake's cocky expression faltered just a bit. The surprise attack from my mother hadn't achieved the desired effect.

That's right, fucker. And watch what I do to you when this is all done.

That's when Audrey started prattling on her delusional bullshit. "I can't believe what you put me through, baby boy. I got fired, my friends deserted me, no one wants a part of me. *I'm ruined.*" She even managed a tear and sniffle, timed with perfect precision, of course. *Bravo.*

In the past, that display of emotion would have moved me. Now, I felt nothing, entirely apathetic towards the scene that played out like a cheap stage show.

And Audrey could read it—my hesitance and revolt.

She shook her head in false disappointment. "You've left me no choice, baby boy. You've left me no choice."

"I've heard those words before, *Mother*," I spat. "And that didn't quite work out for you last time, did it?"

Audrey blanched before taking a step towards me.

"Uh-uh." I tsked. "You sure you want to add assault to the list as well?"

Jake gripped her elbow, guiding her backward to take control of the situation. "Ethan, we have an ultimatum for you."

Great. I can only imagine with the whole cloak-and-dagger performance they've got going on. "Well, spit it out."

"You're going to resign from the NFL. Today will be your last game. And to ensure your compliance, you will announce this at the press conference that we've organised in your name."

One beat. Two. *They're serious. What in the fucking fantasy world?*

I was reluctantly impressed by his delivery. He said that with confidence, no stutter or hesitation. *Good for him, 'cause I'm going to tear him to shreds.*

A dominant smile took over my face, soon bending into a grotesque killer grin as I released a dark chuckle.

"Oh, this is *good.*" I began a slow clap, the rebound echoing off the bare walls. "And here's *my* demands. If you both don't turn and leave this room *right now*, I'm going to show you the real definition of *ruination.*"

Jake squared his shoulders as if he could take me, and Audrey gave a minute flinch but chose to remain by his side.

Hmm, no takers? They'll soon learn.

My gaze caught on Jake's as I chose to address him first. Latent satisfaction bubbled forth as I relayed my threats like a seductive promise.

"I'm going to get you kicked out of football, then blacklist you from the sporting world *entirely.* And every time you try to crawl your untalented, second-rate ass out of the loser hole you came from, I'll be there. To remind you of your place. To push you back down to where you've always belonged... *beneath my feet.*"

Then, I flipped my attention to Audrey.

"And *you.* You've breached your restraining order, which is a criminal offence. But I'll give you this choice as one last gift to the person that birthed me... You can pick between prison or a mental hospital 'cause we all know you're fucking crazy!"

Audrey began screaming like a harpy while Jake held her back.

Then, the door opened, and a random woman casually walked in as if the whole scenario was normal.

"What took you so long?" Jake snapped.

"This place is a damn maze. Take them," she said, handing over an ominous manila folder.

At that, all three pitched their attention to me. That's when I got a clear view of the newcomer, recognition sinking deep as I clocked her origin. She was the influencer in the bar who recorded and released the viral video, Katy.

"What now?" I grumbled, taking them in.

"Baby boy, after all these years, you still haven't learned."

"And what life lesson do you have for me now, *Mother*? Pray tell."

"To love is a weakness—one that can be exploited and used against you."

Why did her words feel like a damning fortune? Like she was the executioner ready to drop the axe on my neck.

That's when realisation whipped through me, frigidly cold and blistering as my faculties shut down one by one. During the turbulent commotion, I had forgotten the reason I agreed to enter the room to begin with, Jake's initial remarks slipping my mind.

The repercussions monumental and irrevocably catastrophic.

"*What have you done?*" I whispered to the three harbingers ready to deal out my fate.

"What is necessary," Audrey said. "You will comply with our conditions, Ethan."

"Or what?"

"Or we will ruin Alicia Thorne... Your Runaway Girl."

Chapter 28
ETHAN

I barked a cocky laugh, concealing the panic creeping up my throat.

Put on a show, Ethan. The best fucking performance you've ever done in your life.

"Now, let me get this straight," I said with false bravado. "Poor pathetic Jake here wants my position. Mother dearest is getting paid for the trouble of causing mayhem. But what's in it for you?" I asked the influencer, her expression faltering beneath my evil-eyed scrutinisation.

I clucked. "Ahh, a typical clout chaser, am I right? You know, you don't have to sleep with him to become something. He can't even make first-string without the use of blackmail."

I winked as her face drained of colour.

"And now what?" I asked, raising my arms wide to address my audience. "You think I'm just gonna step aside while you rip the flesh from my bones? Just because you know who my girl is? *Think a-fucking-gain.*"

I moved to push past them when Jake slapped the manila folder on the lone desk, pictures scattering over the surface with technicoloured finesse.

My step faltered—her beautiful face shining up at me like a pleading promise.

Photo after photo was discarded on the hard surface, each dropping like a loaded grenade, ready to detonate my heart.

Alicia straddling my lap in the front seat of my car… Taken the night I found her crying outside her work building.

Alicia having dinner with Jake, their heads leaning together as if they were conspiring lovers… I recognised her outfit and the setting. It was the same dinner I had overheard her shut him down.

And the worst of all—me staring at Alicia with guilty eyes, stroking her bleeding brow as she looked up at me in anger… The time I accidentally hit her in the head with a football.

They were all taken out of context and staged. Shot from an angle that didn't reflect the reality in front of the lens.

Though I knew what others would see when they looked upon them, the image those locusts were trying to sell. That Alicia was sleeping with her clients, and that I was abusive.

Even so, I didn't care about me.

All I could focus on was my girl and how those pictures would blow up her life. She would lose her anonymity, lose her privacy, and the worst one—her career.

That was one of the main reasons we kept our relationship under wraps for so long. I'd seen firsthand how hard she worked, how much time and effort she had invested into her position. There was no greater loss that I cared about, even when faced with the threat and severity of my own downfall.

I had to protect her.

In that interview, I had proclaimed to the world that nothing else mattered if I didn't have her... *And I meant it.*

"Time's nearly up, baby boy. What is your decision? We have more photos, and you know what we will do if you refuse."

Yeah. Release those images and let the masses fucking annihilate my girl. And no matter how fast she was, she couldn't run away from that.

My jaw clenched, my teeth straining from the added pressure.

"When's the press conference?" I asked, my tone laced with frustration and rage.

"Now—"

I didn't deem them with a reply, instead storming out the door, away from the demons demanding my soul. They didn't follow, knowing I'd probably fucking kill them if they did.

My mind was spinning. There was no time to think. No time to figure out a plan.

It may have been stupid—impulsive, even. But with the proof right in front of me, I couldn't think of an escape without Alicia becoming collateral damage.

I had to prevent that at all costs.

I turned down one corridor, then the next. Blindly finding my way through the underground maze, searching for the conference room that was going to be my end.

Until a lone mirage appeared right before me. A favoured dream—one I always searched for and wanted.

As if she could sense my attention, my desperation, my eyes, Alicia turned, her face lighting up as I ventured closer.

We were on our own, the light reprieve allowing me to breathe for the first time since I entered the stadium.

Within seconds, Alicia launched into my chest as I caught her against me. My heart pummelling behind my rib cage from the mere contact of having her nearby.

Our foreheads met as our eyes drank into one another. My hands raised to bracket her face, imploring her to stay—to remain in that space created just for us.

"You came?"

Alicia gave a cheeky smile. "Of course I came. *I came for you.*"

That's when I pressed forward, my mouth capturing hers in a desperate, yearning kiss. And as soon as my lips touched hers, my resolve solidified into granite.

"*I love you,*" I whispered. Despite the quiet declaration, those three words held the power of the almighty sun. And just like that star, Life would be unsustainable without her in it.

So, I repeated those words like a mantra, chanting them into creation where they always should have been.

"I love you." I stole her gasp by caressing her tongue with mine. *"I love you."* I reverently chased her flushed cheeks with my seeking mouth. *"I love you."*

Each kiss was reverent. Every touch was meaningful.

We were utterly consumed by one another when I heard the distant rumblings of a crowd, my name carried through the air like the slice of a blunt knife.

I gave myself a second, one more beat to soak in her gaze, then reluctantly detangled.

As I went to pull away, she called out in hesitation. "Ethan, what—"

I cut her off with a quick peck. Then left her behind.

I didn't look back. Didn't even spare a glance. And with each step away from her, I knew I was making the right decision.

Alicia was worth it—*she* was worth *everything.*

Chapter 29

ALICIA

I walked into the stadium with faux confidence, discreetly wiping my sweaty palms down my brand-new skirt, trying to shake off some of that pent-up anticipation.

However, a subtle smirk crept through when I thought of my family's reaction to Ethan's tell-all interview.

Immediately after, my hands were shaking so hard I failed to type out a legible message on my phone.

"Here, give it to me!" Alexis dived, making a swipe for the device, and missed.

"Get away from me," I said, holding it out of reach.

"What are you going to text?"

"I don't know!"

Dad grumbled from the corner. "Maybe you should say goodbye, like he asked."

All eyes swung his way when Mum gave a disappointed huff. "Now, Phil."

Two words that had my dad cowering. Then, Alexis thought that would be the perfect opportunity to push her agenda. "Better yet, don't message! Go in person and surprise him, Ali! Oh, my, we *need* to go shopping, get you a killer outfit and a matching teddy to go underneath." She finished with a wink.

"I want a teddy," Austin implored.

"Not that type of teddy, baby."

Dad choked. "Ah, make it stop! Quick, Harriot. I think I'm having another stroke."

"I told you not to eat that chocolate," Mum clucked.

"It's not the chocolate! It's my d-damn daughter's talking all *l-lewd* in front of their sick father." He flopped back on the couch, an arm dropping over his eyes. "See, I'm even stuttering my words. Call an ambulance."

"What's *lewd* mean, Papa?" Austin asked, and Dad just groaned.

Alexis tried and failed to hide a chuckle. "It's an adult word."

"Well, I'm going to ask Cooper. He knows everything." He was referring to his best friend, who had the best ears and an even bigger mouth. The kid boys were dynamite and ignited trouble wherever they went.

My sister sobered. "You're not going to ask Coop. I told you it's an adult word, Austin."

"Fine. I'll ask Coach Owen instead. Then, can we get him a teddy as well, Mama?"

I fell over laughing as Alexis blanched.

Dad gave a defeated sigh. "Cancel the ambulance, Harriot. Just let me die."

There was no question about where us siblings inherited our dramatics. But despite the chaotic scene, Alexis still ended up getting what she wanted.

I didn't message Ethan and chose to reach out in a way that made the most sense to *us*—the unofficial ritual that had become *ours*. Which meant I had to wait until his next game.

It had been a long week, and I was desperate to see him and watch him play. I was so keyed up and bursting with nervous energy that I had to take a breather down a deserted corridor before I fainted from hyperventilating.

That was when I sensed him.

It was as if the forces had worked their magic to intertwine our destinies. Ethan Harris materialised before me, answering the direct call from my seeking heart.

"You came?"

Our passion clashed together as we reconnected after so long.

"*I love you,*" he repeated, sealing each monumental vow with a kiss.

I was lost for words and had altogether lost my mind as I willingly *drowned* in him. My flesh was burning from his touch, scathing with the need for more.

His love was a promise. A reckoning. One beautiful catastrophe. Yet, I'd fight through anything just to remain in that moment.

All too soon, he pulled away, our chests colliding as we caught our breaths.

That's when I clocked the gleam in his eye. A minute conflict that he tried to push down, but could never hide from me.

I attempted to question him. To have him stay in that little piece of paradise we had stolen for ourselves. Yet, he chose to turn away.

A sinister, knowing took hold as I kept my distance and followed him to the press conference.

Although, the instinctive warning wasn't for me. It was for him, my love.

Like everyone else, I wanted to know why Ethan had called a press conference before the game. *There must be a significant reason.*

I slipped through the double doors and pressed my back into a dark corner, the position giving me a clear view of the entire room.

The atmosphere was abuzz, media outlets swarming closer to the stage in an attempt to siphon some of Ethan's fame and energy. He was trending online again. *Everyone* wanted a piece of him.

Not anymore. He belonged to me—every strength, each flaw, they were *all mine.*

A static hush fell over the crowd as the man in question swaggered up on stage to stand behind the podium.

Ethan looked strong and intimidating, but I could sense a hesitance in him. I traced the lining of his shoulders and the way they tensed. As if his mind and body were in opposition.

Then, for a brief moment, his eyes zeroed in on someone near the exit, and his spine snapped ramrod straight.

No one else caught the hint. No one else knew him well enough to notice the tell.

My gaze locked on the culprit at the same exact moment Ethan said the earth-shattering statement that had the crowd in uproar.

"I'm resigning from the East Coast Cyclones and NFL altogether. Tonight will be my last game."

Anarchy ensued.

And as I fought to get to his mother, I made a call, my ear pressed firmly against the phone to drown out the noise.

She answered on the first ring.

"I need your help."

Chapter 30

ALICIA

I could hear the rumbles of the passionate fans, their screams shaking the concrete foundation as I tracked the troublesome trio through the underground corridors. Their auras were easy to follow since they were toxic and pitch fucking black.

Worry and urgency had me overtaken ever since Ethan had dropped the bomb about his resignation.

My bullshit radar was popping off. And I wasn't going to rest until I found out how those three vultures sabotaged my man. There was no other explanation.

"Breathe, Alicia. You got this," Stella said, her tone calming through the phone.

As soon as she had picked up my call, I gave her the quick rundown in sixty seconds flat. And just as I predicted, Stella laid out the harrowing repercussions for Ethan breaking his contract. He would lose millions of dollars and be sued for the rest. The split-second decision was going to change the trajectory of his life forever, and I wasn't about to watch him crash and burn without attempting to save him.

I hummed in the phone, trying to distract myself from spiralling. "So... what if, *hypothetically*, you found out that a certain employee from your company was in a relationship with a client?"

"*Hypothetically*, they'd be fired." *Shit. Shit. Shit.* "But if it's *you*, I'd say there's always a loophole."

I nearly collapsed. "Really?"

"Well, I'm certainly not going to terminate you. And Felix wouldn't dare, with the knowledge you have."

The mention of my boss had prickles skating over my skin.

"Stella, are you okay?" I asked hesitantly. We never spoke about that night I found her husband with his secretary, but I could sense the tension at work. I knew something was brewing behind the scenes.

Stella gave a stagnant pause before answering. "No. I'm not okay. But I will be."

"I'm always here if you need anything," I said. And I meant every word. She didn't reply, but I could feel the promise settle between us.

That's when I saw my opportunity arise. Katy, the influencer, broke away from Jake and Audrey, veering for a bathroom around the corner. I'd recognised her immediately since she was the one who created and broadcast the Runaway Girl hashtag. She was a beautiful woman—a shame she was monstrous in real life.

Tallying the odds, I knew my best bet was to corner her alone. One-on-one was definitely better than going up against three. Especially since they were all delusional.

Stella quietly agreed and placed herself on mute so she could listen and record everything that transpired. For me, it was an added security in case I ever went missing. *Or if I had the sudden inclination to cut a bitch.*

Sneaking into the bathroom behind Katy, I checked that we were alone before I flipped the lock.

When she came out of the stall and saw me standing by the sink, Katy didn't look surprised, just smug. Which pissed me the fuck off.

"What have you done to Ethan?" I seethed. *So much for cool, calm, collected.* My pulse quickened, anger causing my heart to pummel in my chest.

Katy settled beside me, washing and drying her hands as if she didn't have a care in the world. "I don't know what you're talking about."

I took a threatening step forward. "Watch it. Ethan taught me how to throw down." *More so in between the sheets... But she didn't have to know that distinction.*

"I'd be careful if I was you, *Runaway Girl*. Unless you want the whole world to know who you are."

I snickered. "Is that it? You're going to release my identity? Do it," I said with gusto before leaning into her face. "Yeah, you might gain some traction online and boost your reach, but I bet I can steal that. I'll gain more followers than you within the first twenty-four hours."

I didn't care for social media, and sure as shit didn't want my name released by that cretin. But I knew I hit a nerve when her face morphed into a cruel grimace.

"Not with the photos I've got of you! No one would respect you if I released those since you just look like the typical fame whore."

"The hypocrisy is mind-boggling, truly," I sighed. "And I don't appreciate the *lewd* accusation." *Hah, Dad will be proud.*

"I don't care. Our plan worked. Now, you don't want to test me, Alicia. These photos can bring about your demise, not just Ethan's."

A shrill giggle snapped through the air, the noise making us flinch unaware. I slipped the phone out of my pocket and raised it between us, the loudspeaker on full volume. Stella had unmuted herself.

"Who is that?" Katy asked, fear peeking through for the first time.

"Our lawyer," I mouthed, pointing to the screen that displayed the ongoing call.

Katy's expression froze, her eyes bulging with awareness. *Yes, bitch. You've been played.*

Stella's titter tapered off, followed by a voice so sugary sweet it had the underlying venom to rot you to your core. "Blackmail and coercion? *Oh, honey*, that's a *felony*."

"Felony?" Katy choked.

"Let me spell it out for you really quickly since those morons have led you astray. A felony is a serious crime that can result in more than one year in state prison."

"Prison? No, that can't be. I just took some photos. That's all I did!"

Stella clucked. "If you release those photos, you're committing extortion, Katy. That's up to four years in prison and a $10,000 fine. Add on invasion of privacy and emotional distress, and you're looking at a lawsuit that'll destroy your image, your bank account *and* your future. You still want to play this game, honey? Because I promise you, *we'll win*."

Katy was shaking, her hands buried in her hair as she silently screamed into the void.

"What do I do? What do I do?" she repeated, utterly lost.

Stella hummed in fake sympathy. "You're going to do exactly what I tell you to do."

Chapter 31

ETHAN

I stood in the middle of the field, soaking in their praise as they chanted my name. It was monumental—a core memory I would cherish forever.

I'd played the best I ever had in my life—which was fitting. The perfect sign-off to my pro league football career.

It was weirdly cathartic as my teammates hit me on the back, simultaneously giving their acclaim and condolences whilst sporting confused expressions.

One didn't have to guess what was waiting for me once I stepped back into reality—a logistical nightmare to begin the process of dismantling my world.

So I refused to move, choosing to steal a moment to bask in the warm appreciation of the fandom—that I'd never get to experience again.

In that moment, I had no hate, no qualms or resentment. Just acceptance of my decision.

That's when a waterboy came running towards me. He was the only one brave enough to approach and penetrate my bubble. But he didn't hand me a drink. Instead, he gave me my phone.

As I went to question him, he was already retreating when the device started buzzing.

My screen was overrun with messages from Alicia.

The familiar sight caused a pleasant nostalgia to rise, a particular happiness that only she could ever conjure.

Our ritual. I missed her commentary, her snide remarks and sarcastic barbs. What better way to finish the night than check in with my lucky charm.

I swiped open to the message thread and read each one in turn.

> Do you want to give me a heart attack? Because you nearly succeeded.

> How dare you kiss me like that and leave me hanging.

> WHAT THE FUCK ETHAN. YOU ARE NOT LEAVING FOOTBALL!

> Your mother is a rat. Jake is scum. And Katy is a snitch.

That last one had me on high alert, my fingers shaking as they tightened around the phone. *If they've gone after Alicia, I'm going to fucking kill them.*

I held up my end of the bargain. Now, it was time they followed through with theirs by leaving my girl the fuck alone.

Then, a new message pinged through.

Look up, Superstar.

My gaze flipped upwards as I took in my surroundings. I was alone on the gridiron, an abnormal hush taking over the arena as the Jumbotron transitioned into a live feed of the car park.

My eyes widened as I processed the image on the gigantic screens.

Jake fought against three police officers as they tackled and restrained him. Katy sat in the backseat of a cop car, silently sobbing while trying to hide her face from the cameras. And the grand finale was my mother, Audrey Collins, struggling and screaming as she got placed in handcuffs.

"Do you know who I am?! Bring me my son! Get your hands off me. Ethan!"

Even then, in front of an audience, she was entirely deranged.

Overzealous applause invaded from all sides as everyone witnessed my mother and her two accomplices get arrested.

How is this real?

That's when anxiety began to creep in, threatening to drown out that pesky hope that dared to form.

Please be real. Please be real.

I was pulled back to the present, as one heeled foot stepped out of the shadows. Beneath the beaming light, Alicia was immediately coated in a golden halo.

Everything fell away. In that moment, all that existed was *her*.

Alicia gave a tentative smile as her eyes sunk into mine across the expanse. A single moment, a stagnant beat in time was all it took for our souls to stitch back together.

My arms automatically opened, granting her access, begging for her acceptance. *Run back to me, love. I'll catch you.*

Her features flared with recognition before a beautiful grin spread over her face. Then, she ran. Full-speed. Towards me.

Alicia vaulted into my chest, and my flesh sparked from the blissed contact. "You do all this, love?" I asked, tilting my head to the screen, now displaying the cop cars departing with their prisoners in tow.

She gave an innocent half-shrug. "I cornered Katy and struck a deal. We made her squeal on the others in return for a lighter sentence."

I stared at her, frozen, in complete awe of my powerhouse of a woman.

Shock quickly took over. "Shit! Your job. Ali, let's go inside. We can come up with a plan to tell Felix."

Alicia ran her hands up over my shoulders, causing a shudder to run down my spine. "Fuck Felix. And fuck the job."

"Ali?" I didn't want her sacrificing anything for me. I never wanted to take anything away from her again.

"It's fine, Ethan. I mean it," she said with complete sincerity.

My eyes began to burn from her public declaration as all my past insecurities and feelings of inadequacy were immediately sated.

My nose dropped to the base of her neck, wanting to hide my vulnerability since I was on the verge of breaking down. "You saved me, love."

"You saved me first, Superstar." Alicia palmed my face until our eyes caught, tears gathering in both. "You were going to give it all up for me?" she asked, her voice scratchy and hoarse.

I shook my head, in disbelief that she didn't know my heart already. Then, I repeated the same words that were forever ingrained in my soul. "*I love you, Alicia. Nothing else matters if I don't have you.*"

Alicia pressed closer until her lips hovered before mine, the minute touch igniting a heatwave beneath my skin. "*I love you, Superstar*. How could I not?"

Then, in front of the cameras, in front of the crowd, in front of the entire world—I claimed my Runaway Girl, kissing her with the full belief that I was finally worthy of love. *Her love.*

Epilogue

ETHAN

It was over for her.

Alicia thought she was funny, teasing and winding me up with her light kisses and filthy words.

My cock had been solid since I saw her walk out in that luscious black dress, I immediately wanted to rip off my three-piece suit and have my way with her.

Of course, she didn't let me, spouting something about ruining her makeup despite her being the most beautiful woman in the world without it. But that excuse didn't fly since I was now sitting through this torturous award show as if I gave a shit about who the next MVP was. Sure, I was in the running, but I already knew the quarterback had it in the bag.

We sat at a crowded table, champagne in hand, surrounded by some of the best in the game, yet all that consumed me were thoughts of burying myself between Alicia's thighs.

It had been half a year since our relationship was publicly broadcast on national television, and everything had been a whirlwind post.

The three stooges received everything I threatened them with. Audrey was sent to prison for her ongoing unhinged behaviour, and for breaching her restraining order. Jake was let go with a warning, but his reputation was irrevocably ruined, and he was iced out of the sporting world altogether. Katy was also released but was essentially cancelled online and everywhere else, losing all credibility and prospects.

Despite that mess, Alicia and I had had six glorious months together where we constantly made love and loved each other without reservations or any fear. She was my person, my other half, and I was so blissed out that everyone was sick of me. I didn't care.

And just like every other time I thought of my girlfriend, my mind shifted into dangerous territory—how I was going to peel her out of that sleek fabric as soon as we got home.

It seemed my little minx could sniff out my weakness as she leant over, all innocent and whispered in my ear, "Do you remember those pink vibrating panties you sent me when you were trying to win me back?"

I gulped, pivoting closer. "They were a gift to replace the dildo you told me to go fuck myself with."

She released a tipsy giggle, which had my nerve endings short-circuiting. "Hmm, so thoughtful, *Superstar*. I couldn't let them go to waste, now, could I?"

Alicia slipped her palm in mine, transferring a small device into my safe-keeping.

Gods, please be what I think it is.

I peeped the tiny remote, placing it in my pants pocket whilst discreetly readjusting myself.

Alicia then downed the rest of her champagne, sent a cheeky wink and veered for the bar.

Oh, no. She did not just drop that bomb and expect to escape unscathed. Alicia had miscalculated one vital fact when choosing to play with me—*I play dirty.*

ALICIA

Oh. My. God.

I didn't know what I was thinking. *Scratch that—I knew.*

My goal was to tease my man. That by the end of the night, he would be feral and crazy for me.

Although I had achieved my goal, I'd also screwed myself over in the process.

Despite it only being thirty minutes, that remote was Ethan's new favourite toy, and he had no qualms about playing with it every chance he got.

The vibrating panties were deliciously sensual, as I politely conversed with his peers at our table—while my pussy pulsed beneath my evening gown, screaming for the extra stimulation that only Ethan could provide.

Fast. Slow. Fast. Slow.

Every time he pushed me closer to that peak, he abruptly pulled me back from plunging over the edge.

The back and forth had me out of sorts, my fingers quivering on the stem of my glass as a smouldering heat gathered to my centre.

"You alright, love? You look a bit *flushed*," Ethan murmured into the side of my neck.

The minute impression from his lips had me glitching, that I chucked all decency out the window and buried my face in the base of his neck to whisper, "Take me home, *Superstar. Take me home, please.*"

"Mm, I like it when you use your manners. But the show isn't over yet, Ali girl." He finished by subtly poking his tongue out to lick over my fevered skin.

I flinched, scrambling out of my seat—ready to blow, have a violent outburst, or break down in tears. Either way, it was going to be a catastrophe if I continued to be *suppressed* any longer.

I didn't excuse myself, instead bolting for the exit without a word, scared that if I opened my mouth, a moan would escape. I heard Ethan behind me placating the table of concerned guests from my abrupt departure.

"I'll go and check on her. She's feeling unwell," he rushed before chasing me out of the room.

I turned one corner, then another until I was bathed in darkness. I didn't know where I was going, but I had to escape the claustrophobic environment to let my body breathe from all that pent-up energy.

That's when firm hands grabbed my waist and spun me. My back hit the shadowed wall of a hidden alcove as Ethan invaded my front, creating a hidden cocoon from the outside world.

Our chests collided as his arms braced the wall on either side of my head. My eyes raised to clash with his baby blues that were swallowed by the stark blackness of pure lust.

"Are you frustrated, love? Need some relief?" *Pulse. Pulse.*

That little plastic device held all-consuming power as the vibrations sent desire soaring through my body.

I nodded, silently imploring him to touch me.

"Let me take care of you, love," Ethan murmured, his breath fanning over my face with wanton promise.

I hummed in agreement, raising my hands to tighten in his shirt—which he wasn't having.

Ethan clucked, removing my grasp, and anchored my wrists above me so they couldn't go roaming. "You wanted to play, Ali. *So let me play.*"

His fingers were intertwined with mine, and I could feel him press the trigger on the remote to increase the frequency of pleasure throbbing through my apex.

I thrust my hips and writhed before him, searching for that extra friction. He didn't let me, his gaze lapping up my desperate movements as he refused me access, always staying *just* out of reach.

My eyes closed. *Please. Please. "Please, Ethan."*

"Please what?"

"*Touch me.*"

"Mm, I don't think so."

My whine was cut off when Ethan shifted his firm leg between mine, his knee pressing against my centre, creating that blissful pressure that I'd been begging for.

"I love watching you, Alicia," he panted, his eyes blazing as I rubbed on him with rhythmic movements. "To see you is to want you. And with just one taste, I always hunger for more. But when I feel you tonight, I want to take my time and worship your body like you deserve."

Ethan dropped his head, kissing behind my ear, whispering promises that had me unravelling at speed.

"You're driving me crazy, love. Look at you—my beautiful, sexy, confident girl. *Fuck*, all I can think about is burying myself inside you."

"Yes," I hissed, trying to pull on the iron grip he had on my hands. Ethan didn't relent, choosing to press closer to align his front with mine.

"No, Ali love. If you put your hands on me, I'll lose control and ravish you right here and now. I won't care who sees. I'll demand your cries of pleasure, those intoxicating moans, the way you scream my name. *God*, I don't want to risk sharing you with anyone. Because those all *belong to me*."

My teeth burrowed into my lower lip in a poor attempt to suppress the groans trying to rip out of my throat.

"*Superstar...*"

"That's it, love. You're safe. You're protected. You're mine. *Let go.* I'll take care of that pretty pussy, and I'll take care of you, *always.*"

His lust-filled voice and dirty words mixed with the ongoing vibration from the panties had me so completely undone that I climaxed.

I bit hard into Ethan's neck, my shriek getting caught in his flesh as he wrung out every last drop of pleasure by rocking his knee back and forth over my sensitive clit.

"I love you," I mumbled, my body slumped on him for support so I didn't collapse to the floor.

Ethan palmed my cheek until my face was lifted to his. He kissed me, eyes open and gleaming with genuine happiness. "I love—"

"—and the Most Valuable Player is Ethan Harris!!" The speakers boomed, followed by enthusiastic applause.

I smoothed my hands down his suit jacket, entirely sated and happy. "Congratulations, Superstar. You won."

"I already did."

Epilogue 2
ETHAN

Shit. I was nervous.

The Thorne women had ventured out for an afternoon of shopping, which left me alone with Phil and Owen.

"You alright, bro?" Owen asked, pitching an eyebrow. "You look jittery."

We sat in lawn chairs in Phil's backyard, watching Austin play pretend pirates as we chilled with a beer.

Well, *they* chilled. I was overheating by the millisecond. That's when Phil pivoted his attention my way, eyes scanning my bouncing knee.

"Got something to say, Harris?"

I opened my mouth, but nothing came out besides a husky cough that morphed into a choke.

Alicia and I had been together for two years, and in that time, her parents had slowly warmed to me. They loved my dad and regularly met up with us in the city, but I could feel that lingering hesitation.

Like they were waiting and watching to see if I would continue to show up for their daughter. And I did, every single time.

Officially, I was in my last year of football, ready to settle down and find a new normal with my girl.

With Alicia, everything felt easy. That connection had always been there, but with each passing day, it became more potent, raw and unyielding.

After our tragic separation and having a glimpse of what my life could be like without her. I never wanted to experience that again, so I never stopped trying.

I strived to do better and constantly worked on improving myself. *For her.*

And now I had come to the crossroads that every respectable man had to take. It was intimidating, that one question playing on repeat in my mind the whole four hours we drove to Acacia Falls from the city.

What if he says no?

I couldn't let that happen. Alicia loved her father and respected his opinion. I needed his approval and craved it desperately.

"Ethan?" Phil asked, clinking his beer against mine.

That's when anxiety took over, and I blurted, "Phil. I want to formally ask you for permission to marry your daughter..." It was rushed, not at all how I had rehearsed it.

One beat turned into two as Phil just stared at me, his gaze tracking down my frame as if cataloguing each imperfection.

I gulped but rallied with fake confidence. My expression was earnest, portraying that it is what I wanted, above all else on earth.

And just to sweeten the deal, I pulled the offering from my pocket, extending his favourite chocolate bar between us.

Phil's mask cracked before a wide grin took over. He snatched the candy, then pulled me upright into a tight bear hug.

I sagged with relief. "For a second there, I thought you were going to say no."

Phil retreated. "I was never going to say no, Ethan. You're my son. Have been for a while now. As soon as Alicia accepted you into the fold, so did we. She loves you, so we love you."

"Th-thanks," I said, my voice thick with emotion.

"Pay up," Phil said, his palm open in front of Owen, who groaned before swiftly depositing a $50 note in his hand.

I sniggered. "You made a bet?"

"Owen thought you'd pussy out," Phil said.

My eyes narrowed on the man in question, which had Owen raising his hands in surrender. "Hey. I was sure you'd ask, just not *when.*" Then, his features altered into a cheeky smirk. "Better watch out, though, Ethan. Once you put that ring on her finger, you automatically turn into Alicia's bitch."

And I'd have it no other way. Alicia could boss me around, relay her commands and I'd happily follow through like a well-trained pup.

Phil whacked the back of Owen's head. "Watch how you talk about my girls."

My phone vibrated in my pocket, and I smiled when I saw my dad calling. He had met a special lady friend through his fishing club and had gone for a weekend getaway out on the water.

I slipped away to answer and gave him the good news of Phil's acceptance. After a solid ten minutes of Dad relaying his latest catch, I heard female mutterings carry over from the porch. *Alicia's back.*

As I went to wrap up my call, Austin's young voice cut through. "Aunty, guess what happened! Daddy gave Papa lots of money, then, Papa hit Daddy on the head."

"Why'd Papa hit Dad?" Alexis asked.

Oh, no. They warned me the kid had a big mouth, but I didn't expect him to be that preceptive.

As my dad continued to ramble over speakerphone, unaware of my critical situation—I ran over to the porch, ready to shut that little shit up.

Unfortunately, I was too late.

"Daddy said Uncle Ethan will be a bitch when he puts a ring on your fing—"

"Language," Harriot snapped.

"What the hell, Owen?" Alexis said.

Everyone spoke over each other as raucous laughter came through my phone.

Fucking great.

Palming my device over to Phil, I ignored and dodged them all, tentatively approaching a frozen Alicia. Her gaze tracked my every movement.

Once in front of her, I immediately admitted defeat and gathered to one knee, pulling out a ring box from my pocket.

I hummed, then licked my lips. *Why is my mouth so dry all of a sudden?*

"Alicia. This isn't what I had planned. But, in the grand scheme of things, I guess the end result would still be the same. I want you to be mine in every way, and I want to give you that in return. Be my forever love. Marry m—"

"Yes!" Alicia launched right at me. We were caught in a spell of our own making, kissing and hugging and squeezing so tight we were basically one entity.

The Thorne family congregated around us, conveying their congratulations and best wishes towards our shared union.

I kept Alicia next to me, an arm settled around her waist as she showed off her ring. I needed her touch, to make sure I was anchored in this moment of reality.

Owen gripped my shoulder. "Congrats, bro. We finally outnumber the girls. Maybe this means we'll stand a chance?"

"I wouldn't speak too soon..." Alicia whispered, hesitancy coating her voice.

That caught my attention. "What's up, love?"

Alicia stared up at me with glistening eyes, two bright beams of hope shining through. Everything faded into the background as my world was entirely narrowed down and encapsulated onto the woman before me.

Ever so slowly, Alicia grasped my hand and pressed my palm flat against her lower abdomen. A sudden warmth rushed through me as my lungs seized from the deliberate statement.

My baby. *Our baby.*

"Are you happy?" Alicia asked, tears freely running down her cheeks.

I rushed forward planting my lips on hers before I dropped to my knees once more, my face buried in her stomach to try and staunch the onslaught of emotions. "Happy? I never thought this would happen for me, love." I peppered kisses over her middle, loving on my girl and our little creation.

Then, after a long minute, I looked up at my fiancé, freely giving her my tears and my joy beaming from within. "You gave me a family, Ali. You *are* my happiness."

We were shortly surrounded by *our* family, accompanied by Rudy Harris sniffling through the phone. I was one lucky son of a bitch. Enveloped by so much love that I was near bursting with gratitude.

Through Alicia, I had found the future I had never dared to hope for but dreamed of all the same.

She was my purpose. My future. A distant wish, come to life.

Raising to stand, I shifted and pressed my forehead against hers, then whispered one last vow over the seal of her lips. "Thank you for running back to me, love. Thank you for giving me this life. *Thank you.*"

Also by V. Brown

Temple of Kings

Godless Creatures

Soulless Deeds

Sin & Redemption

Mercy Lake

Runaway Girl

Medical Malpractice

Due Process

About the Author

V. Brown is an avid reader whose wild imagination could not be contained. She soon fell in love with writing, creating worlds where anything is possible.

Emergency nurse by day and writer of all things dark and steamy by night, you can usually find V sitting on her back porch with a cup of tea and a good book, surrounded by Australian wildlife. Her husband, daughters and pet chicken named Shadow are always close by.

Stay Connected

Printed in Dunstable, United Kingdom

75310458R00100